Montgomery Lake High #3
The Aftermath

Written by Stacy A. Padula

Edited by Michael Mattes

Briley & Baxter Publications | Plymouth, Massachusetts

ISBN: 978-1-7331536-7-6

Book Design: Stacy O'Halloran

Dedicated to Anthony Padula

Prologue

Jason Davids glanced at his bedroom clock. Seven nineteen. Twenty-four hours had passed since one of the darkest moments of his life. He sighed and fell back on his unmade bed. He curled into the fetal position and tried with all of his might to will the horrifying image out of his mind.

He had not slept a wink in thirty-seven hours. He glanced at his clock again. Seven twenty. *You can do this Jason*, he urged himself silently. *Just get up and go. Go tell them the truth. Tell everyone at Alyssa's party that you found Andy's body. Tell them that he looked dead. Tell them about the horror in Chantal's eyes when she came rushing up the stairs. Make sure you tell them that it is entirely your fault.*

Jason heard a loud knock on his bedroom door. "Jay-dawg, you ready?" Luke's voice cried out. "We have to pick up Laurelle and Missy on the way," he added as he whipped open the door.

Jason sat up in his bed and rested his head in his hands. "Yeah," he replied to his older brother. "I'm good."

"You're going to Alyssa's party in a t-shirt and sweatpants?" Luke asked as he sat down at Jason's desk and stared at him with amusement.

"Oh," Jason said and glanced down at his attire. The thought of getting dressed had not even occurred to him. "No, I guess I'm not."

Luke laughed. "What drug are you on right now?" he questioned him.

"None," Jason stated flatly and stared blankly at his feet.

"Then what the heck is wrong with you?" Luke asked.

Jason shrugged.

"All right, well, get dressed and come downstairs when you're ready," Luke said, eyeing Jason with a look of concern.

Jason nodded slightly.

"Did you sleep last night?" Luke pressed him.

"No," Jason admitted quietly.

"You and Cathy all right?" Luke asked, holding his stare on Jason.

Jason shrugged.

"Well, freshen up. I'll see you in a few," Luke stated. He tossed something at Jason as he exited the room.

Lifelessly, Jason glanced at the minuscule bag of white powder that had landed beside him on his bed. If he had the energy, his eyes would have protruded from his face in horror. "You have got to be kidding me, Luke," he heaved, shaking his head in dismay. He flung the bag onto his floor, fell back on his bed, and closed his eyes. *You can do this, Jason. Just get dressed and get out the door, right now. Bring out the charm and the plastic smile. Forget what Cathy said. Just get up and face the facts. You've made a mess of a good person's life. You have to tell them the truth. It doesn't matter what Cathy wants. Andy is all that matters now.*

Chapter 1

***

Three Weeks Later

It sounded like a train coming toward him, but there was not a train in sight. A flash of light shot through the room—the capsule. Was this a time warp? Or, perhaps, a flashback? Running—more running without getting anywhere. "No, Chantal! Stop!" he screamed. His words froze in the air.

She could not hear him. Time was running out. She was running toward the staircase with her long auburn hair flowing into Jason's face. Watching, he knew that she was not going to make it before the trembling began. She fell over before he could reach her. Once again, he had let her down.

The light flickered, and he struggled to remain standing. He reached the stairs, but did not stop by Chantal's side. The door ahead looked like a castle wall—a barricade. The other side held the destruction. The other side possessed the danger. This door—his enemy—was keeping them safe.

"Jason, don't!" Cathy's voice cried out. She did not sound like his fifteen year old girlfriend; she sounded like a hissing demon.

He latched onto the doorknob as it transformed into a vault. It looked like his locker. His mind was blank. *I can make this right*, he thought. He pressed his hand to the door. It was a glacier. Water began trickling through his fingertips. He felt completely alone. A crackling sound above caught his attention. *Wake up, Jason!* he screamed at himself. *Wake up before you see him. Not again.*

In an instant, Andy's pale face appeared through the water. Jason's heart pounded. "Trade places with me!" Jason pleaded as he reached out toward Andy. There was a crash, and then Andy was gone.

Breathing heavily, with sweat dripping down his forehead, Jason shot his large blue eyes wide open. "Again? Really?" he said aloud in the stillness of his dark bedroom. He brought his hand to his chest and breathed in deeply. He turned toward his alarm clock. Three thirty-three a.m. It had been three weeks since the storm had struck Montgomery, since Andy had slipped into a coma and since

3

Jason had realized that he was living in a cloud of darkness.

* * *

Later that evening, Jason sat upon the bleachers behind Montgomery Lake High School, leaning back comfortably and paying little attention to the JV football game in front of him. Surrounded by the popular MLH underclassmen, Jason continuously yelled obscenities at everyone who was not his friend. As usual, this caused obnoxious laughter to erupt from the crowd and embarrassment to burn within the innocent passerby. Each time Jason got a reaction out of someone, his friends gave him props, which only egged on his tactless behavior.

"Yo, dude! Is Luke really dating *Missy Kent*?" Nick Chandler, a sophomore, asked Jason. "I've heard some things."

Jason shrugged carelessly. "I have no idea, dude," he replied after taking a sip of vodka and Sprite from his soda bottle.

"Your brother's the man, dude. Seriously," Nick stated and slapped Jason's hand before walking over to a group of junior girls.

Jason glanced toward the field. *Where's my boy?* he thought as he shot his eyes from left to right, looking for Chris Dunkin. *Coach Mitchell wouldn't rest his star running back—not against Lincoln North.* Jason looked toward the scoreboard. *7 to 3, us.* Glancing back at the field, he saw Bobby Ryan throw a long pass toward the end zone. *There he is. He catches; he runs; he scores!* "Woot! Woot!!" Jason yelled loudly as the band began playing MLH's touchdown song. Jason turned to slap hands with Bryan Sartelli. "If Chris had gotten sober before tryouts then he probably would have made varsity," Jason commented beneath his breath as he turned back toward the field. "My brother should pull him up."

"Let's go back to Luke's car. I need a refill," Bryan said. He waved his empty coke bottle in the air, stealing Jason's attention away from the field. "I don't get many nights like this without 'you-know-who'," he added and rolled his hazel-brown eyes. Jason assumed that Bryan was referring to his overbearing girlfriend—the mayor's daughter—Courtney Angeletti.

"Ha!" Jason laughed as he rose from the bleachers. "Let's peace-out. Luke wanted to go to Samson's anyway. You can do a lot more than booze out of a soda bottle with that crew."

4

"All right. See you guys later," Bryan called loudly and nodded toward the large group that they had been sitting with.

"Yeah, later," Jason said as he glanced at the field before descending the bleachers.

"Let's grab Anderson," Bryan suggested.

"Where is that kid? I haven't seen him since we got here," Jason asked as he paused to peer through the crowd.

"There he is!" Bryan called out.

Jason followed Bryan's gaze and spotted Jon standing behind the cheerleaders with Katherine Rossi. "Ha! Of course, he's talking to grade-A quality. He never lets us down."

"He's *so* sweating that girl," Bryan said with a laugh as he stepped in front of Jason.

"He's ridiculous to think that he has a chance with her," Jason stated. "She's here trying to watch her boyfriend play, and Jon's here trying to score points of his own."

Bryan shook his head and laughed. "He's the champ! I wouldn't discredit the possibility."

"Tru-dat," Jason sang and flicked the visor of Alyssa Kelly's baseball hat as he passed by her.

"Hey, guys!" she cried out with a bright smile. "Where are you headed?" She was sitting beside Marielle Kayne, who was wearing Chris's football sweatshirt.

"Oh, hey," Bryan said as he turned to face the girls. "I didn't see you there."

"Hi," Marielle said quietly. Jason noted the suspicious expression on her face as she glanced at Bryan's empty soda bottle.

"We're grabbing Anderson and then heading out with my brother," Jason stated and nodded toward Jon. "What are you ladies up to tonight?"

"You're not staying to watch the game?" Marielle asked. "Chris is playing so hard out there!"

"Obviously!" Jason exclaimed. "He's winning the game for us. I don't need to watch the whole thing. I have faith my boy will pull through." Jason turned away from Marielle and took a sip of his drink.

5

"We'll catch you girls later," Bryan said as he jumped down a row of bleachers. "Have a good one."

Jason waved goodbye, without making eye contact with either of the girls, and followed Bryan down the rest of the bleachers.

Chapter 2

"Jessie? Hello? Are you even listening to me?" Sarah Gleeson exclaimed and snapped her fingers in front of Jessie Robin's face.

Jessie turned toward her best friend. "Sorry. What were you saying?"

Sarah sighed. "I swear you only wanted to come to this game because *he* would be here."

Jessie dropped her jaw. "How could you say that? I don't even know *him*, and *he* certainly doesn't know me!"

"He's a jerk!" Sarah exclaimed as she glanced at the group of freshmen boys standing behind the cheerleaders.

"Don't be judgmental," Jessie said and blushed slightly. "You don't even know him."

"Um, okay, sorry to be sinful—or whatever—but, seriously, have you ever listened to him talk? He's not a nice person!" Sarah cried out defensively. "I know your dad's a pastor, but how can you not judge someone like *that*?"

Jessie rolled her eyes and turned away from Sarah. As she glanced toward the field, a magnetic-like force captivated her eyes and planted them upon *him*. Dressed as nicely as usual, in a pair of khakis and a loose blue sweater, he stood out from his crowd of beautiful people. Doing some sort of jig—most likely making fun of someone nearby—he had his friends in hysterics.

"I'm sorry, Jessie. I don't want to discourage you. I'm just trying to look out for you," Sarah said apologetically. "I know that you think he's cute, but he's *bad news*. You don't even want to go there! Plus, he's dating *Cathy Kagelli*. She's the last person anyone should cross. She and her friends would rip you apart."

Jessie's heart sank at the sound of Cathy's name. It was hard to believe that Cathy had once sung alongside her in church and slept over her house. "I'm not afraid of Cathy," Jessie stated sternly. "And it's not that I think Jason's cute. It's nothing like that at all! I've told you a million times; God is drawing me toward him."

7

Sarah laughed. "Why in the world would God draw you toward someone like him? Did you tell your father? He'll straighten you out. Listen to me, Jessie. There is no way God wants you to have anything to do with *Jason Davids*. He's like the Satan of our grade."

"God's ways are not our ways," Jessie replied as she glanced again in Jason's direction. "I know God's voice, Sarah. Just pray for me."

Walking in front of the bleachers toward a large group of juniors, Jason pulled his vibrating cell phone out of his pocket. For the fifteenth time that night, he sent Cathy's call to voicemail. *What does she not understand about a break? It's not a breakup, so there is no need to freak out!*

Their "break" had taken place five days prior. Since then, she had called him over fifty times and refused to speak to anyone except her closest friends, Lisa Ankerman and Julianna Camen. It bothered Jason to see Cathy hurt, but he knew that he could not help her, unfortunately, until he found help for himself.

Chris made it look so easy. Chris had been worse into drugs than Jason, and he had practically given them up overnight. Chris had even admitted that getting sober had been easy for him. Most importantly, he had said that he would help Jason. Dating Cathy pulled Jason away from Chris and into everything detrimental to his life.

Chapter 3

"I'm going to get hot chocolate," Jessie stated and rose from the bleachers. "Do you want to come?"

"Of course," Sarah replied and stood up beside her friend. "I'm all set with sitting here by myself. I don't even care that we're winning."

Jessie laughed. "Well, thanks for coming with me. My dad said that he has a 'friend' on the team that he'd like me to cheer on," she said, walking across the bleachers toward the concession stand.

"Who's your dad's friend?" Sarah asked with a short laugh. "No one from youth group is on the team."

"You're going to laugh when I tell you," Jessie replied. "You'll think I'm making it up."

Sarah rolled her eyes. "Try me."

"Number 85—Chris Dunkin," Jessie said and widened her eyes.

Sarah laughed. "Okay, you're kidding right? How does your father know *Chris Dunkin*?"

"You haven't noticed a change in Chris?" Jessie questioned her as she stepped down the stairs toward the field. "He comes to church now. He's been coming since September."

"I saw him at Andy's prayer service, but I also saw Jason, Lisa Ankerman, and Leslie Lucus. I just figured Chris was there to support Chantal, like the rest of them," Sarah replied.

"I don't think I'm supposed to tell you this, but you probably won't believe me anyway," Jessie said as she stopped on one of the steps and turned toward Sarah. "Chris and Jason came up with the idea for Andy's prayer service."

A perplexed expression coated Sarah's face—the exact reaction Jessie had expected. "I'm not budging. Jason's still evil," Sarah stated and stepped past Jessie down the remaining steps.

Jason and Bryan walked to the right of the bleachers where Luke and his friends were gathered. Luke was standing with his girlfriend against the chain-linked fence near the concession stand.

"Sup, Jay?" Luke called and waved Jason over to him.

"We're ready to leave when you are," Jason replied as he walked toward Luke with Bryan. "Hi, Missy."

"Hey, Jay," Missy said. She flipped her long blonde hair over her shoulder and smiled brightly. "Your bestie's playing really well out there tonight."

"Yeah," Jason agreed and glanced back at the field. "Chris is sick."

"I'm down to the last beer I brought in," Luke stated as he patted down the cargo pockets of his khakis. "I'm good to leave in a few. Why don't you guys go get us some pizza?"

"Dude, what are we? Your slaves?" Jason asked and rolled his eyes.

"Hey! You owe me," Luke said and pushed Jason toward the concession stand. "I'm about to take you to the sickest party you've ever seen. Saddle up, cowboy."

Jason sighed and reluctantly turned back toward the bleachers. "Yo, at the party, I'm staying clear of any blunts that get passed around," Jason said quietly to Bryan as they walked toward the concession stand. "You can do whatever you want, but I'm good with it."

"Is Luke still going to give us those painkillers?" Bryan asked.

"Eh, maybe. He doesn't like me taking pills, but I think I convinced him to give me a few," Jason replied. "Hopefully, he'll be buzzed and not care."

"Well, either way, don't worry, dude," Bryan said. "I won't be smoking up either. I can't lie to Courtney, and I know that she'll ask if I smoked anything."

Jason patted Bryan on the back appreciatively and then stepped into the food line. He leaned to his left to read the wooden menu above the ordering window. As he turned to suggest pepperoni pizza to Bryan, he felt his eyes grow abnormally large and his cheeks begin to burn.

Jessie was standing in line at the concession stand with Sarah when a group of sophomore boys approached them. From the scents on their breaths and the hazy looks in their eyes, Jessie could tell that the boys were intoxicated.

"Hey, girls. How's your night going?" one of the boys asked as he leaned in closely to Sarah.

Sarah turned away and rolled her eyes at Jessie. Jessie continued to stare straight ahead.

"Oh, what, you don't have any love for my boy?" another one taunted and stepped beside the first boy.

"Can you just leave us alone, please?" Sarah retorted sternly.

"That's tough with two cute girls," a third one laughed as he walked around to the other side of Jessie. "Why don't you come chill with us?"

"Because you're annoying," Sarah rebuked and latched onto Jessie's arm.

"Woah! That's bold!" the first one laughed. "I like the little feisty one."

"Why don't you girls come sit with us for the rest of the game?" the third one suggested and placed his arm around Jessie's shoulders.

"Please don't touch me," Jessie said calmly.

"I don't think these broads like us very much," the third one said to his friends as he tightened his grip on Jessie. "That's just because they don't know how satisfying we are."

Jessie dropped her jaw and turned to push the boy off of her. Before she was able to lift a finger, the boy went flying off of her and onto the ground. Jessie's heart pounded heavily inside of her chest.

"Stay the #$@% away from her!" Jason Davids screamed at the sophomore on the ground. "Don't either of you look in their direction!" he cried out as he turned to face the other two boys. He grabbed hold of his fist that had sent Jessie's perpetrator to the ground and turned toward Bryan Sartelli. Bryan's eyes were wide, and confusion was plastered all over his attractive face.

11

"Oh, what, do you think you're tough or something, Davids?" the boy on the ground called out as he wiped blood off his lip.

A large crowd began gathering around them as people started chanting, "Fight! Fight!"

Suddenly, the boy on the ground jumped up and lunged at Jason, thrusting him into the chain-link fence nearby. Immediately, Jason wrestled him to the ground. The sophomore's two drunken friends jumped in, dragging Jason off of their friend and pinning him up against the fence. Without hesitation, Bryan lunged at the sophomores, grabbing one of them by the throat and punching him across the face.

Luke Davids, the most handsome boy at Montgomery Lake High, appeared through the crowd. His normally-at-ease disposition turned angry once he caught sight of Jason being choked up against the fence by two of the boys. Without a second of hesitation, Luke tore the boys off of his younger brother. "What the hell is going on here?!" he screamed as he thrust the two boys into the crowd and then separated Bryan from the other one.

Gasping for air, Jason leaned against the fence with his eyes closed.

"Don't you know enough to stay away from *my* brother?" Luke yelled at the bloody sophomores who were fleeing the scene.

"I started it," Jason huffed, gasping for breath as he opened his aquamarine eyes.

Jessie stood frozen, trying to process the scene before her.

"What was the heck was that about?" Bryan asked as he eyed Jason warily. "Dude, you sucker-punched O'Leary for no reason. What the hell?"

Luke and Bryan stared expectantly at Jason as he slowly stepped away from the fence. He began walking toward Jessie, brushing dirt off his sweater. "Are you okay?" he asked, panting and eyeing her with concern.

Jessie swallowed deeply and nodded, gazing hesitantly into Jason's glassy eyes.

"All right. I have to get out of here before the principal shows up, but I'll see you around, Jessie," Jason stated and smiled at her before hustling off through the crowd.

Jessie stared blankly ahead as the world spun around her. She blinked, half expecting to find herself sitting on the bleachers beside Sarah, realizing the fiasco had been a mere daydream. That, however, was not the case. Jason not only knew who she was but also felt the need to protect her—two things she had never expected. "I'm not even thirsty anymore," she stated. She let out a short laugh, realizing that she had underestimated God.

Chapter 4

"Okay, you need to run that by me one more time. Who is that girl?" Bryan asked as he jogged beside Jason toward Luke's car.

"Her name is Jessie Robins," Jason replied, stopping short at his brother's BMW 650i black convertible. "I really don't want to get into it. She's just a girl in our grade. O'Leary was being an idiot. No one should treat a girl like that."

Bryan stared at Jason skeptically, recalling the many times one of their friends had mistreated a girl and Jason had done nothing but laugh. Clearly, Jason had some ulterior motive for fighting O'Leary. "Well, I think she's pretty cute," Bryan said.

"She's do-able," Jason stated flatly.

Bryan laughed. "You're going to have to explain this a lot better to Luke. He seemed pretty heated," Bryan said as he noticed Luke and Missy heading toward them.

Jason rolled his eyes and touched the small cut on his cheek. "Good thing I planned on popping Vicodin tonight," he said as he twisted his bruised wrist. "It's eight o'clock, and I'm already banged up. God help me."

"What are you doing to celebrate tonight?" Justin Knight, the captain of the team, asked Chris Dunkin inside the locker room.

Chris smirked. "I am, first and foremost, thanking God for our victory and then chilling with my girlfriend at the Kagellis' house," Chris replied as he stood up from the bench.

"No crazy booze-fest?" Justin asked and stared at Chris strangely.

"Nope," Chris laughed, wondering if his old reputation was going to haunt him for the remainder of high school. He patted Justin on the shoulder and walked toward the exit.

"Wow, you really do take more after Marc than Jordan or Taylor," Justin said with a short laugh, referring to Chris's older cousins—Montgomery Lake High football legends. "Ha, well good game, bro. See ya at practice."

14

"Later," Chris called as he tossed his gym bag over his shoulder and exited the locker room.

It would be so nice to see you smile, Katherine Rossi thought as she watched her boyfriend Bobby Ryan walk out of the locker room. She had been waiting for him in the gym with her close friends Lisa Ankerman, Leslie Lucus, Jeff Brooke, and Adam Case for fifteen minutes. She knew that everyone was trying to pretend Andy was outside, just in the bathroom, or on the bleachers with Chantal. Sometimes, the mind game actually worked, the self-trickery, the delusion of it all. *That's not really an empty seat at our lunch table. Andy is just in line, getting a drink.* But he wasn't. He was in a hospital bed across Montgomery, hooked up to machines, fighting for his life.

"Hey, guys," Bobby greeted them. He let out a loud sigh once he reached his friends. "I'm exhausted."

"Good game, hunny!" Katherine exclaimed, hoping that her excitement would somehow be contagious and steal Bobby out of his sullen mood. She jumped up and threw her arms around him without hesitation.

"Yeah, Dunkin carried the team—again," Bobby said. He dropped his gym bag to the floor and squeezed Katherine tightly. "That kid's unstoppable."

"You made some good passes, man," Jeff said from behind Katherine. "We were watching."

"Any word on Andy?" Bobby asked as he set Katherine free from their embrace.

"Sorry, dude," Adam said and shook his head. "We haven't heard anything."

"We'll go visit him tomorrow," Lisa assured Bobby and placed a supportive hand on his shoulder. Katherine leaned against Bobby's other shoulder as they began walking out of the gym.

Chapter 5

"Can you guys believe that I'm taking my little bro with us to Samson's? Ha! Jay-dawg! This is going to be *fantastic*," Luke exclaimed and laughed loudly over the EDM that was blaring from his car stereo. "Oh man, I was a sophomore when Matt started taking me out with him. This is going to be intense. You're what, fifteen?"

Jason rolled his eyes and nodded. "Dude, I've been partying with you guys since I was twelve. I don't think anything could shock me at this point," he stated dryly.

Luke laughed. "Matt's there already, tearin' it up. I'm sure he's going to be pumped to see you. That's so wrong, isn't it? That we look forward to corrupting our little brother?"

"You guys are terrible," Missy said and slapped Luke's arm playfully. "Leave poor Jason alone."

Again, Jason rolled his eyes. He shook his head and turned to face Bryan, who was sitting beside him in Luke's backseat. Jason knew that Luke was trying to embarrass him in front of Missy. Luke knew exactly what Jason was like when it came to partying. *Great,* Jason thought, *just when I wanted to take it easy, my brother had to go and challenge me.*

After the football game, Jessie stood with Sarah inside the vestibule near the gym, waiting for Mr. Robins to pick them up. Typical of any Friday night, Jessie was having Sarah sleep over. However, the girls would have normally gone to youth group instead of a JV football game. Jessie's father had cancelled youth group unexpectedly that night and suggested that she attend Chris's football game. His father-like heart toward Chris had taken Jessie by surprise. She had only found out about Chris and Jason's involvement in Andy's prayer service from her father's secretary, Rachel. Before that, Jessie had had no idea that Chris had even met her father. Hearing her father call Chris his "friend" had made Jessie's stomach flutter. To think that her father wanted her to become friends with Jason's best friend encouraged Jessie.

Something seemed to be tying Jason into her life.

God had pointed Jason out to Jessie the week after the tornado struck Montgomery. Jason had suddenly looked beautiful to her, like the most beautiful person she had ever seen. For most freshmen girls, that would seem like common sense. Jason was someone whom "every girl" found attractive. On the contrary, Jessie had never found Jason attractive. His relentless taunting, crude remarks, and conspicuous interest in controlled substances had tainted his physical appearance and rendered him completely repulsive to Jessie. So, seeing him suddenly look beautiful had caused Jessie to nearly fall off her seat.

After that day, she had begun asking her friends, "What did Jason Davids do to himself? He looks really different." They would all reply with something along the lines of, "What are you talking about? He's always looked like that. He's gorgeous!" That was when Jessie had begun earnestly praying *about* and *for* Jason. Three weeks later, standing in the gym's vestibule with Sarah, Jessie's curiosity about Jason was at an ultimate high.

"I feel kind of bad about the things I said earlier," Sarah admitted softly and hung her head. "That was nice of Jason to stick up for us. He didn't have to do that. I don't understand why he did? We don't even know him."

Surprised by Sarah's humility, Jessie opened her mouth to respond but quickly swallowed her words. Lisa Ankerman, Leslie Lucus, Katherine Rossi, and their boyfriends were entering the vestibule: the class beauty, drama queen, and snob all in one pack—as usual. They were the *last* people Jessie wanted to mention Jason's name in front of. Lisa was one of Cathy's best friends, and Leslie had the biggest mouth in the entire school.

"Hi, girls!" Leslie greeted them, waving and smiling brightly as she stepped toward the vestibule's exit. "Have a good night."

"Thanks," Jessie and Sarah replied in unison.

Lisa glanced at them, rolled her eyes, and flipped her long chocolate hair over her shoulder. She latched onto her blonde-haired, blue-eyed, model-like boyfriend, Jeff Brooke, and tugged him out the door. As Katherine stepped out the door, she glanced over at Jessie and Sarah and pursed her lips before turning back toward her boyfriend, Bobby.

Sarah and Jessie let out heavy sighs of relief once they were alone in the vestibule. "I *cannot* understand how *Andy Rosetti* is best friends with those people!" Sarah stated dramatically as she leaned against the wall. "Andy is so nice to everybody, but his friends are such snobs! Did you see the look Lisa gave us? She's his best friend! I don't get it."

Jessie shrugged. "Don't you remember how different Andy was when Chantal first brought him to youth group? Then he *suddenly* changed into this perfect guy when she agreed to date him. Remember? I assume Andy has a side to him that the public doesn't see. People make him out to be flawless, but everyone has flaws. Yeah, he's charming, but he never comes to church without Chantal; he doesn't usually come with her to youth group; and he doesn't engage in fellowship. I try not to be judgmental, but I worry that he only comes to church to please Chantal. Andy just gives me an uneasy feeling."

"Really?" Sarah questioned Jessie and tilted her head to the side. "Andy's one of the nicest people I've ever talked to. He plans fundraisers for all those charities and talks to adults so comfortably. Almost two thousand people showed up for his prayer service—that should speak volumes! Don't you think you're being a little judgmental, Jessie?"

"I'm not trying to be," Jessie replied honestly. "It's just a feeling I get—a vibe he gives off. It doesn't sit right with me. I want to believe Andy is a sincere person, but I can't."

"Ha, well you get a good vibe from the class *drug dealer*!" Sarah exclaimed in an amused manner.

Jessie rolled her eyes. "You can't believe *every rumor* you hear about Jason! People just assume stuff about him because he's so outwardly wild at heart. I'm not saying he's innocent by any means. I'm sure he was drunk tonight, and I know he's a pothead; but look at Chris! He was *way* worse of a troublemaker than Jason, and now he's the star of the JV football team and evidently 'friends' with my father! People change when God calls them."

18

Sarah crossed her arms. "Whoever said God was calling *Jason Davids*?" she asked and threw her arms up in the air. "He punched a kid who was being a jerk to us, so now you think he is being called by God? What is wrong with you, Jessie?"

Jessie rolled her eyes and shook her head. *Why did I even mention Jason? I shouldn't expect Sarah to understand.* Silently she made a pact with herself to never again mention his name. If someone brought him up, she decided that she would shrug and say that she didn't know him. That seemed feasible, right? Unfortunately, she had underestimated the brutality of high school gossip.

Chapter 6

Driving past the fifty-plus cars that lined the street, Luke pulled his BMW into Samson's driveway and parked behind his older brother's Lexus GX 470. One benefit of being Matt Davids' brother was a reserved parking spot at every party. "So, Jay-dawg, you wanted a few of these?" Luke asked, shaking a prescription bottle before Jason's eyes.

Jason nodded and quickly snatched the bottle. "My wrist is kind of banged up from the fight. Can I have the rest?" he asked and popped off the plastic top to count the pills.

Luke eyed Jason warily. "I got those for some kids in my grade. Just take what you need for tonight and leave the bottle," he replied. "And be careful; I don't want to clean up your puke later," he added.

"Fine," Jason sighed and poured five pills into his hand.

Luke reached into the glove compartment for a second prescription bottle. "This is for us," he said and winked at Missy.

Jason observed the excited look on Missy's face. "What are you taking?" Jason asked and raised his eyebrows curiously.

"No. You're not touching this," Luke stated sternly and tossed the bottle into his cargo pocket. "Let's go."

It was unlike Luke to take any type of drug. Jason wondered if Missy's wild ways were starting to rub off on his older brother. Luke used his connections in Boston to get drugs for his more rebellious friends, which made him quite popular with the juniors and seniors at MLH. Missy, in particular, took full advantage of Luke's drug hookup. Club drugs, like ecstasy, molly, and coke, were her and her friends' forte. More often than not, Luke stayed sober and played babysitter to his girlfriend, who was typically the life of every party.

"Here. Take these. Now," Jason said and handed Bryan two pills before climbing out of the car.

"How many are you taking?" Bryan asked, holding the pills in the palm of his hand.

Jason shrugged. "If I'm not getting high tonight, then I'm

getting wasted." He grabbed Bryan's drink and threw three pills in his mouth. "Ah, delicious," he said and climbed out of the car.

"Wait, but can't you get high from Vicodin?" Bryan asked, still sitting in the car with the pills in his hand.

Jason smirked. "Well, I mean, if you don't have a tolerance, you *can*," he replied, wondering why Bryan had asked.

"Dude, I don't have a tolerance," Bryan said flatly. "What will it do to me?"

"You're not going to get *high* from two Vicodin," Jason replied. "It will just add to your buzz. You'll feel a little bit more relaxed, maybe a little lightheaded—if anything. Crushing them up and snorting them wouldn't even get you high."

Bryan widened his eyes.

"What?" Jason asked with a short laugh.

"I definitely don't want—"

"—Guys! Come on!" Luke yelled impatiently from the top of the driveway.

"Whatever," Bryan said and jumped out of the car. He shut the door behind him, tossed the pills in his mouth, and washed them down with Captain and Coke.

"You'll be fine, guy," Jason said and patted Bryan on the back as they began walking up the driveway. "You'll just feel drunk off fewer beers than usual."

"All right," Bryan said, sounding a bit more at ease. "The first time I take any drug I get nervous. Adding to my buzz is fine; I just didn't want to take too much and end up getting high."

"Understandable," Jason said. *Crap! I should have only given him one,* Jason thought. *Two Vicodin could mess him up. Two Vicodin add to my buzz, but I take this crap all the time.* "Hey, if you start to feel weird, make sure you stop drinking," Jason warned him. "I've taken double what you just took and been okay, but I've built up a tolerance over the last few months. Just be careful."

"Do you take Vicodin so you can drink less and still get drunk? Or do you take it to get high, Jay?" Bryan asked and stopped ten feet away from Luke and Missy.

Bryan's words caught Jason off guard. He hadn't expected Bryan to be so direct; after all, Bryan was his most reserved friend.

21

Bryan's question was one that Jason had asked himself often, so his answer came easily. "I don't want to get high anymore," Jason replied solemnly. "I don't want to take crap up my nose or smoke weed or trip out. I don't want to do half the things I do on a daily basis. I just want to get drunk and forget about Andy's accident and Cathy's insanity for one night."

Bryan nodded. "All right," he said and continued walking toward Samson's house.

Jason and Bryan trailed behind Luke into the party. They entered through the side door of the ranch-style home. Sitting around the kitchen table was a group of seniors whom Jason knew personally: his oldest brother Matt, Ricky Samson, Pat Ryan, Bob O'Donnel, Robby Rosetti, Katie McKnight, Laurelle Mahoney, and Ally Jordan. Matt was wearing an empty thirty-rack box on his head and shuffling a deck of cards.

"Aha! Winning again, I see," Luke teased Matt as he walked by the table.

"JD!" Matt cried and ripped the box off of his head. "Sit down, little bro! We're going to play a game!"

Jason and Bryan quickly grabbed chairs from the dining room and pulled them up to the kitchen table.

"Ryan, grab two of my beers out of the fridge," Matt called to Pat Ryan. "So, *technically* one of you guys is the servant, but, since you're learning, I'll sport the box."

"Why would we automatically be the servants?" Jason asked as he picked up the hand of cards that Matt had just dealt him.

"Oh! Uh-oh! You picked up your cards before the King! You have to drink 'til I tell you to stop!" Samson cried out and pointed at Jason.

"I have no idea what you're talking about but, ha, okay," Jason said and tilted his beer to his lips at a ninety-degree angle.

"That's right, dude. That's my little bro! The best way to learn is by getting thrown right in the fire! Woooo!" Matt laughed and patted Jason on the back.

Jason had nearly finished the entire twelve-ounce can when Samson told him that he could stop. "Okay, people! Pick up your cards!" Samson said without looking up from his hand. "Whoever is the low guy on the totem pole, give me a joker or a queen if you have one."

After an hour of playing the game, Jason still could not make sense of it. It seemed that every five seconds he had to drink, for one reason or another. *I know I'd be better at this game if I could understand the point of it,* Jason reasoned. *I must look like a freakin' idiot! Do the rules keep changing?* Jason looked across the table at Bryan, who had four empty beer cans in front of him. Bryan looked relaxed.

After playing another round and finishing his sixth beer, Jason felt his phone vibrate in his pocket. Although he didn't want to take Cathy's call, it was an excuse to leave the table. His entire body felt light, as if he were floating, and he knew the beer had little to do with it. He was high.

"I'm going to take this call," Jason said and rose slowly from the table. "Deal me in next round, though."

Bryan looked up at Jason with a strange expression on his face. "I'll come with you," he stated and stood up from his seat.

"Hurry back," Matt said and began laughing. "There's plenty more winning that needs to be done at this table."

"Hello?" Jason called into his phone as he slowly led Bryan onto the back porch. He leaned against the railing and struggled to stand on his feet, even after placing one hand on the railing.

"Hey!" Cathy's voice cried out, nearly piercing his eardrum. "I've been wondering when you were going to answer."

"What do you want?" Jason asked flatly. He wiped his sweaty forehead with his hand and then quickly placed it back onto the railing. He gripped it tightly.

"I heard you were at Ricky Samson's party, and I wanted to come see you," Cathy replied.

"Ah, yeah…um…I don't think that's a good idea," Jason stated slowly, suddenly wondering why he didn't think it was a good idea. He felt nausea settling in. "Actually, I'm not feeling too well."

"I can come cheer you up!" she exclaimed enthusiastically. "I could bring you some food or anything else you want."

She sounds so cute, Jason thought. *Wait, we're in a fight.* "I don't know, hun," Jason said with a sigh. *It would be good to see*

23

her. I'd kind of like to just lay down with her and talk. "Let me call you back in a minute," he said and ended the call.

"Hey! Hey!" Luke exclaimed as he stepped onto the porch. His expression grew perplexed as he got closer to Jason and Bryan. "Is he all right, dude?" he asked Bryan.

Jason was pretty sure that Luke was referring to him. *Do I really look that confused about Cathy?*

Bryan shrugged. "He took three painkillers and finished six beers since we got here. Plus, he downed vodka at the game."

Luke widened his eyes and raised his eyebrows. "Oh boy," he said and pulled a pack of cigarettes out of his pocket. "I should have told Matt to go easy on him."

That would have been nice, Jason thought. *Maybe if Cathy comes, she can be my excuse to stop playing that horrible game I completely suck at.*

"It wouldn't have made a difference," Bryan remarked. "Jay's on a mission to get wasted."

"Want one?" Luke asked and offered Bryan a cigarette.

Jason looked at Luke strangely, wondering why he had cigarettes in his hand. Luke didn't smoke. No one in his family smoked. Smoking was disgusting.

Bryan squinted in thought. "Nah, I'm good," he said after a bit of hesitation. "I think I finally quit. You smoke?"

"No," Luke scoffed. "This is an attempt to boycott vaping. It's a long story—don't ask. Who were you just talking to, Jay?" he asked after lighting a cigarette.

"She-devil," Bryan stated and rolled his eyes.

"Cathy!" Luke exclaimed. "You were talking to my little Cathy? Ah, I love that girl! Is she on her way? Jay-dawg! Give me your phone!"

Jason looked at his brother and shook his head.

"Aww, c'mon dude. Let me call her," Luke said and grabbed the phone out of Jason's hand. "She should be here."

Jason stared blankly at Luke. *Why is he smoking? Is he completely wasted?*

"Who's this?" Luke called into Jason's phone ten seconds later. "Ah, Cathy! It's so good to hear your voice. What are you up

24

to?...Well, tell me, why are you hurting me like this? Why aren't you here? Get over here!...Yeah. Come take care of my little baby brother who can't handle a drinking game. He's about ready to pass out."

Jason's eyes widened. *Did Luke just invite Cathy to the party?* "Give me my freakin' phone!" he cried out and pushed Luke backwards into the railing.

"Yeah, grab one of your hottie friends and get over here," Luke said with a laugh. He pushed Jason away from him with little effort. "Jay might get a little embarrassed, though. He'll probably be kissing the porcelain when you get here... Ha, all right... See ya." Luke ended the call and turned toward Jason. "I just did you a favor, little bro," he said and handed Jason his phone. "That girlfriend of yours is hot. When you wake up next to her tomorrow, you'll thank me."

Jason threw his arms up in the air and shook his head. "Dude, you have no idea what you're talking about. She's psychotic."

Luke laughed and flicked his hardly smoked cigarette over the railing. "She's a female," he stated matter-of-factly. Then he patted Jason on the shoulder and walked back into the house.

"$#@%," Jason said with a sigh. He took a seat in a lounge chair and buried his face in his hands.

"It'll be all right, guy," Bryan said and took a seat beside Jason. "You can just ignore her. She'll probably show up with Julianna or Lisa. You won't have to pay attention to them."

Why wouldn't I pay attention to Cathy? I love her. Jason couldn't find words to speak to Bryan.

"Are you pissed at Luke? He's in rare form. I've never seen him so... I don't know... hyper," Bryan remarked.

Jason rubbed his forehead but said nothing.

"He thinks he did you a favor," Bryan added. "You know he loves Cathy."

"My stomach feels weird," Jason said, finally finding words. He leaned back in his chair and closed his eyes.

"That game is ridiculous," Bryan stated in a serious tome. "If we go back in and play, then we *are* going to be puking when Cathy gets here."

Jason sighed. "I, like, don't want to get up. My body feels *so good* but my stomach's hating me right now," he said and looked down at his phone. "Crap, it's only ten o'clock. *Really?!* I'll never live this down if I quit drinking before midnight."

"I don't know how much more I can drink. I'm feeling pretty good right now," Bryan admitted, "but if I drink another beer, then I'll probably get sick."

"Yeah, you don't have to drink," Jason mumbled. "Your brother won't give you a hard time."

"Dude, I'm an only child," Bryan said with a laugh. "How much did you drink in there? You *are* effed up!"

Jason looked over at Bryan, wishing that he had only taken two pills. "Yup, and the night is still young," he said. *Get up. Get up. Get up,* he urged himself. *Get back inside. Matt is waiting for you. Yup. If he ever finds out that you took pills tonight, @#$%! One more round of that game will convince him that you're not a lightweight. He has seen you drink more than six beers before. He's going to know something is wrong with you. He's going to find out about the painkillers.*

"Jay, seriously, are you okay?" Bryan asked.

Jason shut his eyes and ignored Bryan completely. *Focus. Focus. Adderall. Yes, Adderall. Do I have any? Yes, in Luke's car. That will sober me up. That will help me focus on the game.* "I need to go to Luke's car," Jason said and stood up from his chair.

"Why?" Bryan asked. "I thought you wanted to go back in and play the game?"

"ADHD medicine," Jason replied. "It will help me focus."

"Do you really think you should take another pill? You've already put a lot of stuff in your stomach tonight," Bryan reasoned. Jason detected an abnormal amount of concern in Bryan's tone.

"Yeah, you're right. Well, I'll just blow it. That solves that," Jason said and began walking toward the backdoor.

"Jason. Jason? Jason!" Bryan called out as he latched onto him.

The feeling of Bryan's hands on his shoulder startled Jason. He turned around to face Bryan, wondering what was wrong with him.

"No," Bryan stated firmly. "You're drunk. Cathy is on her way here. Listen to me."

Jason was staring at Bryan but finding it hard to focus on his words.

"Jay, you said that you don't want to get high anymore—you are. You said that you don't want to see Cathy anymore—you are about to. You said that you don't want to take stuff up your nose—look where you are headed. Stop while you can. Let's ask Matt to bring us to my house. You can get out of here before Cathy even gets here. Seriously, you don't want anything that this party or Luke's car has to offer."

Jason lowered his eyebrows and swallowed the large lump in his throat. He closed his eyes. *If I leave, then I won't get to see Cathy.* "I want to see Cathy," he blurted out.

"No, you *really* don't," Bryan stated firmly. "You think you do because you're high, but you really don't. Trust me. You *do not* want to see Cathy."

"JD, are you a girl or something?!" Matt exclaimed as he opened the backdoor. "What dude talks on the phone this long?"

"No worries. No worries. No worries. I'm off," Jason said and stepped toward his brother.

"Well, then get back inside," Matt stated, sounding slightly amused. "I was afraid you were smoking weed out here."

"No, no, no, no, no," Jason assured Matt as he followed him into the kitchen. "I don't smoke weed anymore."

"How I wish that were true," Matt commented dryly as he pulled a chair out for Jason. "We dealt you in this round. You ready?"

Jason nodded.

"You sure?" Matt asked.

"Yup. Let's do this," Jason stated as he glanced at Bryan, who was sitting on the other side of Matt. Bryan looked upset, or irritated, or worried, or sick—something. "Are you up for this, Sartelli?" Jason asked and nodded at Bryan.

Bryan raised his eyebrows. "I need to chill for a bit," he replied. "I'm going to put my cards on the bottom of the pile and sit this one out."

27

"No big deal," Samson said. "All right, you guys can pick up your cards now."

Chapter 7

Sure enough, by eleven o'clock when Cathy arrived at Samson's, Jason was on all fours, puking in the bathroom. Bryan, who had opted out of the last six rounds of the drinking game, was struggling to fight off his own nausea. He hated the way he felt. He watched Cathy as she walked into the party with Julianna Camen. Just as Jason had predicted, the girls became instant eye magnets.

Marc Dunkin—Chris's older cousin—and Luke were the first to make their way over to the girls. Bryan remained seated at the table, hoping that he wouldn't have to speak to either girl. Cathy despised Courtney; surely Cathy would use Bryan's intoxicated state to her advantage. That was drama he simply didn't need in his life.

"Where's Jay?" Cathy asked as she peered at Luke curiously.

"Yeah, about him," Luke said with a laugh. "I told you that he'd be yakking by the time you got here."

Cathy nodded. "Well, what did he take?"

"Some P.K.s," Luke replied. "A few, actually."

"He's stupid," Cathy said. She rolled her catlike green eyes and crossed her slender arms. Bryan thought she looked uncomfortable. "Should I go find him?" she asked.

"Well, why don't you hang out for a bit?" Marc Dunkin suggested. He raised his eyebrows and glanced from Cathy to Julianna.

Jason would be so mad at Marc if he saw this, Bryan thought.

Cathy glanced at Julianna, shrugged, and then turned back to Marc. "Whatever," she replied. She looked up at Luke. "As long as you think Jay's okay."

"Ummm…you should probably go check on him," Luke said with a crooked smile. "I'm sure he'd like to know you're here. Your friend can come with us, though."

Julianna's eyes widened. *She looks petrified,* Bryan thought. *Way to go, Cathy. Take the most timid girl in our grade and bring her to a party with Luke Davids.* Julianna darted her eyes at Cathy.

"What?" Cathy asked softly. She lowered her eyebrows at Julianna. "You'll be fine with them! Luke is Jason's *brother*. I won't be long."

Julianna sighed and followed Marc and Luke out of the kitchen.

"Hey, Sartelli," Cathy greeted him on her way toward the bathroom.

"Hi," Bryan replied, grateful that she had not stopped to chat. It would take someone as smart as Cathy about three seconds to realize that he was drunk. That was the last piece of news he wanted getting around school and buzzing into Courtney's ear.

Jason sat on the bathroom's cold floor with his head up against the ceramic tile wall. Sweat poured profusely down his face and he felt like his head was in a cloud. He could barely feel his own hands as he attempted to wipe the sweat from his forehead. For the first time since seventh grade, he had gone overboard.

He began violently vomiting again, wishing that he had never taken a sip of alcohol. The room had transformed into a plane of black and white spots, and it hurt to keep his eyes open. Impressing his brothers had not been worth a single second of the way that he felt. He wanted to curl up in a ball and die. His stomach continued to contract, the room continued to spin, and his body felt numb all over.

"Jason!" Cathy's voice suddenly pierced through his throbbing headache. The doorknob began turning quickly back and forth. "Unlock the door! Let me in!"

Gagging, Jason crawled over to the door and turned the knob to unlatch the lock. Without glancing up at Cathy, he crawled back to the toilet and continued to heave.

"Oh, you *are* really sick," Cathy said compassionately. Jason heard the door shut and lock. He sensed Cathy on the ground beside him. Her hand felt warm on his back. "How much did your brothers make you drink?"

"Can't… talk… now," Jason gagged.

"Do you want me to stay in here with you?" Cathy asked.

"If…you…want," Jason heaved.

30

"Well, do you need anything? Any water? Or maybe some food?" Cathy asked, again rubbing his back.

Jason shook his head and wiped his mouth with the sleeve of his sweater. He sat up straight and then curled into the fetal position on the scatter rug. All he wanted to do was sleep. He closed his eyes. Five seconds later, he felt as if he were somersaulting through the air. Within thirty seconds, he was bowing miserably at the toilet.

"So, Julianna, tell me about yourself," Marc Dunkin said and sat down beside her on the living room couch.

Without Cathy by her side, Julianna felt more insecure than she could ever remember. *How did I end up at a party filled with seniors?* She was petrified of Jason, let alone his older brothers and their friends. "What do you want to know?" she asked, somewhat embarrassed by her apparent timidity.

Marc shrugged. "I don't know. You seem different since the last time we hung out. Remember? I met you at Chris's."

Julianna nodded and swallowed the large lump that had formed in her throat while Marc had been speaking.

"I didn't know that you hung out with Cathy," Marc commented, raising his eyebrows in Julianna's direction.

"I never used to," Julianna replied and hung her head. "We became friends last month…when Jon and I broke up."

"Well, everyone here adores Cathy. So, anyone who's cool with her is cool with us," Marc assured Julianna and patted her leg.

Julianna's heart began racing. "Do you know Alyssa, Lisa, and Leslie?" she asked, wondering if he would touch her leg again. She glanced at his arm and traced his defined biceps with her eyes.

"I know Alyssa," Marc said slowly, "but she doesn't come around anymore. Lisa's the really pretty one who used to date Chris, right? She's a cheerleader?"

Julianna nodded. "Yeah, she's *really* pretty. Actually, all of Cathy's friends are pretty. Leslie's the blonde with the bright green eyes. She's a cheerleader with Lisa."

"Who's their other friend—the little brunette?" Marc asked.

"Katherine Rossi," Julianna replied, admiring the light blue shade of Marc's eyes. "I don't really know her well."

31

"She's cute," Marc said and took a sip of beer. "So, what were you and Cathy up to earlier?"

Julianna shrugged. "Nothing really. We were just hanging out at my house."

"Do you hang out with my cousin anymore?" Marc asked and reached into a nearby thirty-rack. He offered Julianna a beer.

"No, I don't," Julianna replied and took the can from Marc without hesitation. "He's dating my best friend, Marielle, but I don't see them often. They're always with Courtney, and she's still mad at me for becoming friends with Cathy." She rolled her eyes and looked away from Marc.

"That's ridiculous!" Marc exclaimed. "I really don't understand girls. Luke is my best boy, and I don't care who his other friends are! There's no need for drama like that."

Julianna nodded. "I agree, but Cathy would freak out if I hung out with Courtney. So, it comes at me from both directions. They *hate* each other."

"Are you friends with Chantal?" Marc asked.

"Um, no," Julianna replied hesitantly. "Not really. She doesn't have anything against me, but you really have to pick your twin. Obviously, I'm close with Cathy."

Marc laughed. "Well, I think either one is a good pick. Chantal's a really nice girl. She's got the whole package. Cathy is just crazy—but in a good way. I like them both."

"Don't you and Chantal hang out?" Julianna asked, recalling how jealous Cathy had sounded when she mentioned Chantal and Marc's friendship.

"We talk a lot online, and I call her every once in a while. She has a boyfriend, though, so it's tough. I don't want to cross any lines or disrespect anyone—especially with her situation," Marc explained. "Do you know what I mean?"

"I guess," Julianna said. "She hangs out with a lot of guys, though. She's always with Jon. I don't think either of them worries about disrespecting Andy. Jon *so* still loves her."

"Ooh, do I sense a bit of resentment there?" Marc teased Julianna and nudged her playfully.

Butterflies fluttered around Julianna's stomach. *No way,* she thought. *If I were still going out with Jon, then I wouldn't be talking to you.*

"Well, Chantal told me that she and Jon are completely platonic," Marc said. "She said that she knows they were meant to break up in seventh grade. She related it somehow to God."

Julianna's stomach dropped. She felt frustration begin to rise up inside of her. "Chantal and Jon relate everything to God. Courtney and Chris are the same way. They're like a group of Jesus freaks," she blurted out.

Marc raised his eyebrows and stared at Julianna with a perplexed expression.

Immediately, Julianna felt embarrassed by her brash statement. After all, Chris was Marc's younger cousin. "Sorry, did that offend you?" she asked, staring warily at Marc.

"Well, no—not really," Marc said hesitantly. "I just don't think there is anything wrong with people having faith. I actually wish I had more. I might be partial because I think of Chris as a brother, and I've been in love with Michelle Taylor since seventh grade, but people who have faith seem an awful lot happier than people who don't. I commend anyone who has the strength to live their life for God."

"I never looked at it as strength," Julianna admitted. "I also didn't know that Michelle Taylor was a Christian," she added, referring to MLH's Homecoming Queen.

"Have you ever talked to her?"

"No."

"Within five minutes of conversation, you would know."

"Well, I know she's close with Courtney's older sister Day, so that makes sense," Julianna concluded. "Day and her fiancé, John, are really into church. You guys are friends, right?"

"Yeah, everyone in my grade is friends with each other," Marc said matter-of-factly. "I'm pretty tight with John. He and I both usually shy away from the partying scene."

"Yeah, I didn't think you were too big of a partier," Julianna said after taking a sip of beer. After a few weekends of drinking, she was starting not to mind the taste of alcohol. "Jon told me that he and Chris look up to you. I mean, duh, you're one of the varsity football captains! But I think they have more reasons than that."

"Really? Anderson looks up to me?" Marc asked. "He seems strangely standoffish lately."

"Gee, let me think of why that could be," Julianna said facetiously and laughed. "You are friends with Chantal—the girl he's *in love* with!"

Marc smirked. "Well, I do get the feeling that he doesn't like Chantal talking to me. But to get back to the partying thing, I usually fly under the radar during football season. I'm verbally committed to BC, so I can't risk getting in trouble. I'm only here because Matt asked the whole team to come. We only have two more games before the playoffs, and we're all kind of bumming. Some of us have played together since we were Mites. It's crazy to think that next year we'll be spread out on fields across the country."

"Wow! BC! That's awesome!" Julianna exclaimed. "I bet a lot of people are really jealous." *So, he's gorgeous, athletic, and smart.*

"Nah, my friends are all happy for me," Marc said. "They know how hard I have worked for it, on and off the field."

"I'm sure Chris wants to follow right in your footsteps," Julianna assumed.

"I bet he'll get drafted for the pros while he's in college," Marc stated. "I'm glad he's finally focusing on his game. He got way too caught up in partying at way too young of an age. For a while, I thought he was going to throw away his talent for drugs like my oldest brother did."

"So, let me get this straight. You're best friends with Luke Davids, and you're against drugs? How does that work?" Julianna asked, completely dumbfounded.

Marc laughed. "Woah! My wing-man's gained a little rep with the underclassmen, huh?"

"Oh, Cathy's told me *all* about Luke," Julianna stressed.

Marc laughed. "I thought Cathy was a fan of Luke," he said.

"Oh, she's a *big* fan of Luke!" Julianna assured Marc. "If drugs were a turn off to her, then she wouldn't be involved with

34

Jason. She's never said anything bad about Luke; she just told me that he feeds Jason and her pills, whenever they want."

Marc looked taken aback. "He does?" he asked.

"Well...I don't really know," Julianna stammered. "I thought you would know."

Marc widened his eyes. "Luke doesn't say much about Jason, but I'd be surprised to find out that he gave Jason pills. One pill can easily lead to another, and some pills are just as addictive as heroin. What kind of pills did Cathy say she took?"

"I don't know," Julianna replied, deciding that it was time to shove her foot in her mouth.

"I didn't mean to put you on the spot," Marc said, seeming to relax a bit. "I'm sorry about that."

"It's okay," Julianna said, hoping that she hadn't upset Marc.

"Drugs are just a sore subject for me," Marc admitted. "Some of my friends like to dabble in them, but I don't. It doesn't take much for someone to get addicted. I'm pretty sure no one ever intends to become a drug addict. I've just seen it happen too often...to good people."

"People like Chris?" Julianna asked.

"Yeah, and my brother Taylor," Marc said in a somber tone. "My brother threw away his football career, his education, and his relationship with our family because drugs took over his life...I miss my brother...I miss someone who doesn't even exist anymore." Marc paused. He shook his head from side to side. "He's a shell of the person I grew up admiring. He's gone."

"That's terrible," Julianna gasped. "I can see why you'd be concerned about Luke giving Jason and Cathy pills."

"Drugs stole my brother from me, and then Chris got all screwed up," Marc took a heavy breath and shook his head. "I...I can't talk about this anymore."

"I'm sorry, Marc," Julianna said, picking up on the deep pain in his voice. She had never heard someone talk about drugs with such conviction. *Cathy always makes her experiences with pills sound like harmless fun.* "But, thank God you have Chris back. Chris is doing really well. You don't have to worry about losing him," she comforted Marc and gently placed her hand on his arm.

"It's a battle," Marc said. "Chris is going to be fighting it for the rest of his life. He says that God delivered him from his addictions…I believe him…but…that means he will need to draw strength from God every day. There are a lot of things that can get in the way of that—even good things like schoolwork and sports."

"Wait, you really believe that God has something to do with Chris's sobriety?" Julianna questioned Marc, hoping that he was joking.

"I know He does," Marc replied matter-of-factly.

Julianna looked away from Marc. *Really?! Another person who is going to try to convince me to believe in God?*

Marc began laughing.

"Why are you laughing?" Julianna asked and turned back toward him.

"I can just read your expression," Marc said. "You're thinking, 'Great. I came to a party to have a good time, and I'm stuck listening to this kid talk about sobriety.'"

Julianna smiled. "That's actually *not* what I was thinking," she said.

Marc crossed his muscular arms and stared at her skeptically.

"I thought you were going to hurl into a speech about how God changed Chris's life," she explained. "I've just heard it already—a million times—from Jon and Courtney."

"No, I'm not going to do that," Marc said and patted Julianna's shoulder. "The change in Chris speaks loud enough."

"Thank you," Julianna said and glanced at the beer in Marc's hand. "Can I ask you something, though?"

"Shoot," Marc replied.

"Why do you drink if you hate drugs so much?"

Marc looked down at his beer. "Well…like I said…I don't come to parties often," he said after a few seconds. "I'm not here to get drunk. I just like to socialize."

"So, why can't you socialize without drinking?" Julianna pressed.

Marc shrugged. "Sometimes I do," he replied. "Tonight, I felt like having a few beers with my teammates. I think drinking is fine in moderation."

"So, if Chris started drinking again, you'd be fine with it?" Julianna asked.

"No," Marc said flatly. "Chris can't drink in moderation. He's an alcoholic. I'm not. I could take or leave alcohol."

"Well, I guess that makes sense," Julianna said. "It's just weird to be drinking at a party with someone who frowns upon drugs. Most of the kids in my grade who drink also do drugs."

"I know a lot of kids who drink but are against drugs," Marc said and nodded toward the kitchen. "Most of my football team is like that. I just think the freshmen class has a big drug problem."

"Yeahhhhh," Julianna stressed in agreement. "I'd say so!"

"All it takes is for one popular kid to get into stuff, and then it spreads like wildfire," Marc stated. "If only sobriety could spread the same way."

"Do you think Chris feels responsible for my grade's drug problem?" Julianna asked, assuming that Marc had been referring to Chris.

Marc let out a heavy breath. "I think Chris realizes that doing drugs or not doing drugs is a choice people have to make for themselves. He never forced anyone to try anything. I think he feels bad that he introduced stuff to his friends. Thankfully, there are a lot of things he kept from them."

"Really?" Julianna asked. "So, Chris was worse off than Jason? But Jason's head is in a toilet right now! He's a burnout. He blows lines of Adderall! Chris was worse than *that*?!" Julianna could not imagine Chris acting anything like Jason. *Chris treats Marielle with much more respect than Jason has ever shown Cathy*, she thought. *Chris is kind to everyone at school. He's a focused athlete. He doesn't even swear! Courtney and Jon only mentioned Chris's issues with pot and alcohol. I would never correlate him with hard drugs like…wait…what kind of hard drugs?* She felt curiosity rising up inside of her.

Marc nodded. "Chris was much worse than Jason, and that is why his sobriety is a miracle," he replied.

"You don't need to tell me what your cousin was into," Julianna said and shook her head. "Saying he was worse than Jason says enough."

"So, I guess you haven't really heard Chris's story 'a million times,' huh?" Marc teased Julianna and playfully flipped her blonde hair into her face.

"Um, I guess my foot belongs in my mouth," she replied and smiled at Marc. *What gorgeous blue eyes*, she thought. *Cathy, you have my permission to spend the entire night with Jason in the bathroom.*

Chapter 8

A half hour later, a loud knock on the bathroom door broke through Cathy's concerned thoughts. She opened the door to see Matt Davids' anxious face peering at her. She shrugged slightly and then stepped aside so that Matt could see Jason. He had passed out with his face pressed against the toilet seat.

"Ah, what a mess," Matt said with a sigh and stepped past Cathy. "I have to get him out of here. He can sleep in Samson's sister's room. Do you think he can walk?"

Cathy shook her head. "I'm surprised he can breathe," she replied dryly.

"He only had, like, ten beers. I don't get why he's this sick," Matt said and slapped Jason's face.

"Yeah, but Luke said he took a bunch of painkillers," Cathy said and glanced at Jason. "He wouldn't get this sick from beer alone."

"He what?" Matt asked, sounding irate as he darted his eyes up at Cathy.

"He took some pills—probably Vicodin," Cathy replied. "I'm sure he got them from Luke."

Matt shook his head and lifted Jason up from the toilet. "This is crap," he stated angrily. "Hey, Jay, are you with me? C'mon buddy, wake up. Am I going to have to take you to the hospital?"

"The hospital!" Cathy exclaimed and widened her eyes.

"This is my *baby* brother. I'm not going to mess around," Matt stated and tossed Jason over his shoulder. "I'll see how he does lying down."

Cathy let out a loud sigh and followed Matt into a nearby bedroom. Matt laid Jason's lifeless body down on the neatly made bed as Cathy felt nerves begin to rise up inside of her. The Xanax that she had taken before coming to the party had been keeping her anxiety at bay, but the worried look on Matt's face was weakening the effects of the drug. Cathy could not understand why Jason had pushed himself so far over his limit.

"I think he'll be all right, as long as he doesn't choke," Matt commented, still eyeing Jason warily. "I'll send Bryan in here. We can take turns keeping an eye on him. Are you sleeping here tonight?"

Cathy shrugged. "I will if I need to."

"Good. You will probably have to keep checking on him," Matt said. "I can't believe he pulled this tonight. I never would have let him drink if I had known that he was on Vicodin. This is what happens when people mess with drugs. That's why I just stick to beer. Mixing stuff gets you in trouble."

Cathy dropped her eyes to the floor. *I hope Matt doesn't have to take him to the hospital. He will get into so much trouble. His parents will be so upset! They have no idea that Jason does what he does. He's usually so good at balancing everything and limiting himself. Was he trying to drink away our problems? Could he be as upset about our break as I am? Why would he overdo it like this?*

***

Jason woke up early Saturday morning. Blinking, he studied the scene before him. A purple wall, a white lace curtain, and a floral bedspread—nothing was familiar. He sat up quickly and grabbed hold of his aching head. As he glanced to his left, his heart began pounding heavily. He was not alone in the unfamiliar bed. He widened his eyes. *Who did I hook up with last night?* He looked again at the girl who was lying on her stomach. Her head was to the side, and strands of auburn hair were across her face. Jason let out a sigh of relief as he felt his muscles relax—*my beautiful girl.*

He stared at Cathy for a moment and admired her beauty. He wanted to wrap her in his arms and kiss her gently on the forehead. He wanted to run his hand through her long silky hair. Watching her sleep so peacefully almost made him forget how chaotic she was.

Jason sat for a few minutes, trying to recall the previous night's events. He remembered being at the football game with Bryan—oh, and getting into a fight, which explained the throbbing pain in his wrist—wearing a box on his head, playing cards, and…yelling at Luke? Hmmm, strange. None of the flashbacks made any sense to Jason, nor did Cathy sleeping beside him. How had she entered the picture? Whose bed were they in?

Glancing at the clock on the nightstand, Jason widened his eyes. It was only five a.m. Creeping quietly out of bed, Jason escaped from the room without waking Cathy. Tiptoeing down the hallway, Jason stumbled into the wall. Realizing that he must still be drunk, he began wondering how much his brothers had made him drink.

"Woo-hoo! Look at the champ!" Luke cried out and clapped his hands slowly as Jason staggered into the kitchen. "How did the cold porcelain feel against your face, little bro?"

Do I even want to know what he is referring to? Jason thought as he slumped into the kitchen chair beside Luke. With his elbows on the table and his head in his hands, Jason closed his eyes. "How are you *still* awake?" he groaned.

"What's the matter? You don't want to sleep next to your pretty girlfriend?" Luke asked and disregarded Jason's question. "She came here just to take care of you."

"To take care of *me*?!" Jason exclaimed and shot his head up off of the table. "What happened to me? And why do I feel like I'm mad at you?"

Luke laughed. "You overdid it last night. I took a lot of heat from Matt because of you. He just left a couple of hours ago. Matt, Bryan, and Cathy alternated checking on you throughout the night. Bryan's passed out somewhere in the living room."

"What the heck happened to me?" Jason asked frantically.

"The same thing that happened to me the first time Matt brought me to a party," Luke replied with a wide smile. "You puked buckets."

"Ohhhh man," Jason grumbled and threw himself against the back of his chair. "I'm so disgusting. No wonder I feel like crap. How did Cathy end up here?"

"Wow! You really don't remember *anything*," Luke stated and shook his head disapprovingly. "I think it's time to lay off the painkillers, bud."

"Ugh, I forgot," Jason said with a sigh of disgust. He brought his hands to his forehand. "I took Vicodin, huh? I'm such an idiot. What, did I invite Cathy over?"

"No," Luke said and shook his head. "I went outside to smoke, and you were on the phone with her. I stole your phone and told her to come take care of you."

Jason was perplexed; Luke hated marijuana more than anyone he knew. "*You* smoked weed last night?"

Luke laughed and shook his head. "I don't touch weed, Jay-dawg. That's your forte."

Jason eyed Luke strangely. "You smoked a butt?"

"Like, a half of one," Luke replied carelessly.

"Ewe! Since when do you smoke?" Jason asked and puckered his face in disgust. He knew that Luke sometimes vaped, but smoking was completely out of his brother's character. He was the preppiest and most image-conscious person Jason knew.

"You were smoking, too!" Luke teased him.

"Shut up!" Jason exclaimed as a vibe of panic rushed through his veins. "I would never smoke a cigarette."

"I know. I'm *just* kidding," Luke assured him and rolled his eyes.

Jason sighed. "Dude, don't scare me like that. You could tell me that I tried coke last night and I'd believe you. I can't remember anything."

"If you blew lines, then you wouldn't have passed out at eleven-thirty. Rumor has it you drank eleven beers in less than two hours and popped three Vicodin beforehand. Plus, you drank a pint of vodka at the game. What the heck were you trying to do, Jay-dawg? Matt almost brought you to the ER," Luke stated and slapped Jason lightly in the head.

Jason widened his eyes. Not only was he embarrassed, but also ashamed. *So much for taking it easy. Clearly, a pint of vodka changed my mind.* "I didn't smoke weed, did I?" he asked, hoping that he had at least kept *that* promise to himself.

"Nah, no one even had any," Luke replied. "Matt and those guys just stick to beer. They're not drug-bags like your friends."

Jason laughed. "Shut up, dude! You're probably on something right now."

"Probably," Luke said with a smirk. "Hey, whatever keeps my head out of the toilet."

42

Jason rolled his eyes. "Can we go home? Or should I go pass out on the floor?" he asked, allowing his irritation to ring through his tone. His entire body ached, and he'd had enough of Luke's smart comments.

"What do you want to do?" Luke asked as he turned toward his girlfriend.

"I'm crashing, babe. I'd like to go to bed somewhere," Missy replied softly and leaned her head against Luke's shoulder.

"All right, we'll go to my house," Luke stated and lifted Missy up off his lap. "Jay, go wake up Bryan. You should offer Cathy a ride home, too. Her house is on the way."

"No way," Jason replied and shook his head. "I don't want to talk to her, dude. It messes up my head. We're on a break for a reason."

"Ohhhh, so that's why you got pissed at me last night," Luke said. "Yeah, I might have conveniently forgotten about your break."

"Whatever," Jason said with shrug. "I'm sure she'll find a ride home."

"Dunkin shacked up with her friend on the couch. I'm sure he'll offer to drive them home," Luke remarked as he put on his wool peacoat.

"What friend? Who came with her?" Jason asked curiously. *There's no way Lisa cheated on Jeff!*

"I don't know, some skinny girl," Luke replied carelessly. "She seemed petrified of everyone, but Marc warmed her right up."

"Ha, of course. That's the Dunkin trademark. It must be Julianna because she's even afraid of me." Jason laughed as he stumbled across the kitchen toward the living room. Bryan was hugging a pillow and sleeping in a frog-like position on the carpet. *I'm kind of glad I got sick,* Jason thought. *A bed with Cathy certainly beats Bryan's sleeping arrangement.* "Get up, dude," he said softly and nudged Bryan's shoulder.

Bryan shot his bloodshot, brown eyes open immediately. "Yeah, like I was actually sleeping," he mumbled. "Dude, I cannot believe you're awake right now."

"Shhh," Jason hushed. "Let's go before people wake up."

43

Twenty minutes later, after dropping Bryan off at his home, Jason, Missy, and Luke arrived at the Davids'. In the foyer, Luke and Missy rushed past Jason and up the stairs. They were out of sight by the time Jason reached the bottom step. As he climbed onto the third tread, Jason felt his right knee buckle. His left hip slammed into the wall, and he hung onto the railing for dear life. *Don't wake up, Mom. Don't wake up, Dad.* The landing above looked miles away. Dropping to his hands and knees, Jason paused for a few seconds before beginning to crawl toward the second floor. With one hand in front of the other, Jason crawled all the way to his bedroom.

Climbing under his sheets and pulling his baby-blue down comforter high over his head, Jason planted his face into his king-sized pillow. "Why do I do this to myself?" he mumbled, trying to figure out how he had become such a disaster. After a discouraging attempt to sort out his contradictory thoughts, Jason decided it would be easier to ponder in sobriety. Within minutes, he passed out, waking up with cold sweats and dry heaves throughout the day.

Chapter 9

Jessie Robins awoke Saturday morning with a smile pasted across her face. She couldn't wait to tell her mother all that had happened during the football game. Her mother was the only person she told everything to—including her feelings toward Jason. Her mother had been praying with her daily about the situation, seeking God's guidance, wisdom and discernment.

Jessie left Sarah asleep in her bed and hurried downstairs to help her mother prepare breakfast. Mrs. Robins had been making Jessie and Sarah chocolate chip pancakes every Saturday morning for the past five years. Although the sugary breakfast had seemed a bit more appetizing at age nine, Jessie still treasured the tradition behind it.

"Good morning, Mom!" Jessie cried cheerfully as she entered the bright kitchen. "Oh, hi, Dad! I didn't expect to see you."

"Good morning," her parents replied simultaneously.

"I was just grabbing a cup of coffee to take into the study. The kitchen will be yours and your mother's in a second," her father said with a laugh.

"Well, you seem awfully smiley," Jessie's mother commented, while eyeing her curiously. "Did you have a good time at the game?"

Jessie nodded and spread a wider smile across her face.

"Was *he* there?" her mother whispered.

Jessie nodded again and widened her eyes.

"Excuse me, but who might 'he' be?" her father asked and glanced at Jessie.

"No one," Jessie replied quickly.

"God has pointed out a young boy to Jessie," her mother stated and threw her arms around her husband.

"Oh, really?" her father asked as he raised his eyebrows. "And what are your thoughts on this, Mom?"

"I think it's something for Jessie to keep in prayer, and it will be a great lesson of patience and faith," her mother replied as she winked at Jessie.

"Ah ha, I see," her father said. "May I ask who this boy is? Someone from church?"

"Well, no," Jessie stated slowly. "No, not exactly. I don't think you know who he is, but you're 'friends' with his closest friend—a certain football player."

Jessie's father blinked abruptly. He seemed startled by her response. He opened his mouth to speak, paused, and then closed it. "Uh huh, I see," he said after a moment, while wearing a rather puzzled expression. "Well, I'm sure *whoever* this boy is, God has a plan for him, and you will be a light in his world."

Jessie lowered her eyebrows and tilted her head. "You don't want to know his name?" she asked.

"Nope," her father replied with a smile. "But I'll be praying for you both," he added and walked out of the kitchen.

"That was *not* the reaction I was expecting from him," her mother admitted and placed her arms across her chest.

"Me either!" Jessie exclaimed.

Chapter 10

Saturday afternoon, Bobby Ryan stood in Andy's hospital room with his head down. Andy's mother had left the room to give Bobby the chance to confide in Andy. "The doctors said that he might be able to hear," Andy's mother had stated. "Talk to Andy like you would any other day. I think he would like that."

Fighting back tears, Bobby glanced at Andy's blank face and shook his head sadly. "Hey, Andy," he said quietly after a moment. "I'm not sure if you can hear me, but I hope you can. I miss you, guy. We all miss you. They had a prayer service for you a few weeks ago, and *thousands* of people showed up. We all think you're going to be fine, so stay strong. None of us have lost hope yet.

"You're probably wondering how Chantal is doing, huh? Well, you know her. She's hanging in there, staying strong in her faith. She's been keeping busy with cheerleading. Oh, she and Alyssa became friends again. Chantal and Jon Anderson are friends again, too, but I don't think you need to worry about him. I'm pretty sure he's given up on Chantal and is now after Katherine. Yeah, so things aren't too great between her and me. I'm not sure if we'll be together for much longer. I think I am the problem. I'm so depressed; I can't show her much love these days. I feel bad because I know she deserves attention, but I'm on empty. I know if you were awake, you'd have some good advice for me. You'd tell me not to let her slip through my fingers. I know she's a good catch and that I care about her...I just...I don't know... I have little emotion toward anything. I've even been slacking at football. We *did* win last night, but seriously, it was all Chris Dunkin. He's so good; it kind of makes me jealous. I'm just glad he's on my team.

"Chris has actually turned into a pretty good kid. He's still sober and dating Chantal's friend, Marielle. He and Jason Davids came up with the idea for your prayer service, which shocked a lot of people. I think Jason feels responsible for what happened to you, even though it is obviously not his fault. I know that Chris is trying to help him deal with everything. Seriously dude, your injury has brought out the best in so many people. Only *you* could pull off

47

being in a coma and making Montgomery a better place. I miss you, bro. We're all praying for you. Leslie said that when you're better we could go up to her lake house. We'll throw a huge recovery party for you, all weekend long. Her parents said that you could invite everyone you'd like. It will be a *real* good time.

"Leslie, Lisa, Jeff, Adam, and Katherine are all really worried about you. Lisa's definitely struggling. I just keep telling her that you're going to pull through. We both believe that you will. We love you Andy, so keep on fighting the battle. See you soon, buddy," Bobby said and took a long look at Andy before exiting the room.

Chapter 11

The first time Jason woke up without dry heaving was at seven twenty-eight on Saturday evening. Finally, his room had stopped spinning and his body had returned to a stable temperature. *What a waste of a day*, Jason thought as he threw his comforter off of his body. He looked down and widened his eyes. Jumping out of bed, he realized that he was still wearing puke-covered clothes. "Ugh!" he cried and ripped the sheets off of his bed. Within thirty seconds, his sheets were in the hamper, and he was in a pair of Abercrombie sweats and an MLH t-shirt.

Hoping to bypass any family members, Jason crept with his hamper to the laundry room. He didn't want his parents to question why he had refused breakfast, lunch, and dinner, and he certainly was not ready for Matt's inevitable lecture. *Matt must have heard about the painkillers,* he reasoned. *Surely that was the "heat" Luke had referred to.*

Emptying his hamper into the stainless-steel washing machine, Jason began to think about Cathy. It was unlike him to just leave her at a party, especially after she had gone out of her way to care for him. *That was pretty rude of me,* Jason concluded. He hated hurting people, and he was sure that he had hurt Cathy. Unfortunately, he had screwed up too much at the party to allow himself to fall more deeply into his old ways.

He programmed the digital washing machine and selected a clean pair of sheets from the linen closet. Carrying the sheets and his hamper toward his room, Jason noticed a small bruise on his wrist. Between being violently sick, upset about Cathy, and mad at himself, Jason had forgotten about his fight with Sean O'Leary. If Jason had the chance to redo the evening, punching Sean was the one thing that he would *not* change.

As Jason entered his bedroom, he saw Matt sitting at his desk. His heart plunged to his stomach. He made brief eye contact with Matt and then dropped his eyes, along with his hamper, to the floor. He threw the clean pile of sheets on top of his barren bed and took a seat beside them.

"I almost had to take you to the hospital last night," Matt stated, sounding more concerned than angry. "Do you even realize how sick you were?"

Jason looked up at Matt and shook his head. What could he even say to his brother? He had no excuse for acting so irresponsibly.

"Why didn't you tell me that you took Vicodin?" Matt questioned him and threw his arms up in the air. "Did you think I wouldn't find out? I mean, pick your poison! Come on, Jay! You're smarter than that."

Jason sighed and hung his head. "I felt like I had to live up to you and Luke," he said, without making eye contact with Matt. "Plus, I was already drunk when I took the pills. I think I forgot I even took them. I don't know. I can't remember much of anything. Normally, I know better than to pound beer when I'm on stuff."

"You're fifteen years old," Matt stated seriously. "You shouldn't be *on* anything. It makes me so angry to see you following Luke's footsteps. I love the kid, but he hasn't been making wise decisions lately."

Jason scoffed. "You think?"

Matt sighed. "He's been making horrible decisions, and I'm worried about him, but this conversation is about you. *You* are the one Mom and Dad always brag about. You're so ridiculously brilliant that sometimes I'm even jealous of you. Don't mess that up. Ten years down the road, the parties, the drugs, and your high school reputation are going to mean nothing to you. If you felt pressured to live up to Luke and me, then your thought process is messed up. You have surpassed both of us already on so many different levels."

Jason stared silently at Matt for a moment and bit his bottom lip in deep thought. Matt's statement begged the question: why did Jason even bother with drugs? He had intelligence, popularity, charisma, a wealthy family, an abundance of friends, and a long list of girls to date. Without drugs, he would still have all of the above. So, what good did drugs bring to his life?

"Matt, I appreciate your concern," Jason said slowly and looked up at him. "I don't have an excuse to give you. Most people think, 'if only I were popular,' or 'if only my family had money,' or

50

'if only I could get straight A's,' then I'd feel fulfilled. So people set their minds to these intangible things and work toward them. I can't do that because I already have those things, and it makes me really depressed that I'm still not fulfilled. So what do I have to look forward to or work toward? When I smoke weed, or trip, or take Vicodin, I feel good. And even though the fun only lasts temporarily, it is an escape from the emptiness I feel. I know that sounds horrible. I'm so unappreciative of everything good in my life. I can't help it, though. I'm, like, hollow."

Matt stared at Jason thoughtfully. "Well, maybe you should take your eyes off of yourself. Start volunteering or something," he suggested.

"I felt good the day I spent with Chris, you know, putting together Andy's prayer service," Jason admitted quietly and put his head down. "I felt, for once, like my life had a purpose. You know? Like, I was actually valuable to society or something. The best part about that was I didn't do it for that reason. I was really into it. I liked that feeling."

"Then don't let go of that," Matt urged him and smiled slightly. "After Andy's service, did you feel guilty about helping out?"

"What kind of question is that?" Jason asked. "Of course not."

"So, volunteering made you feel good while you were doing it and afterwards, too?" Matt questioned him.

Jason nodded, wondering why his brother was asking such obvious questions.

"And it kind of took away the emptiness that you say drugs take away?" Matt implied.

"Yeah, I guess."

"Well, how do you feel after the drugs wear off?"

Jason widened his eyes, suddenly understanding Matt's point. "Do you even have to ask? Look at me right now. I usually feel worn out, sick to my stomach, and guilty about all of the stupid things I say when I'm not thinking straight," he replied honestly.

"Exactly."

Jason nodded in recognition.

"Good talk, JD," Matt stated and patted Jason on the shoulder as he exited the room.

Chapter 12

Sunday morning, Marielle Kayne awoke between Alyssa and Chantal in Chantal's queen-sized bed. Chantal's house had become Marielle's weekend home. She loved the warm feeling that filled her every time she entered the house. Chantal's parents were amazing people—abundantly welcoming, loving, and friendly. The more time she spent at the Kagelli's, the more she understood why Chantal was such a good person. On the contrary, the less she understood why Cathy was so callous.

The day that Chris had been praying for had finally arrived. One hour later, Marielle would be attending church for the fourth time in her life. Unlike the other three times, she wasn't going for a wedding, funeral, or prayer service; she was going to learn about the God her friends claimed to know.

"Do you think Jon is going to come today?" Alyssa asked as the girls began getting ready.

"Actually, he said he was," Chantal replied.

"It will be good for him," Alyssa said as she peered into Chantal's full-length mirror. "Church simmers his temper."

"I'm really happy you two are civil again," Chantal stated while she lightly sprayed herself with perfume. "It was awesome hanging out here with everyone after the game. It's so nice to have you all in my life again. You don't know how many times I considered going to a party just to see you, Chris, and Jon."

"Really?" Alyssa asked, sounding shocked. Even Marielle was surprised to hear Chantal admit such a thing.

"Well, yeah," Chantal said with a shrug. "Thank God for Andy because I would have been really lonely in eighth grade without him. Cathy had turned on me and away from God. You, Chris, Jon, Bryan, and Jason had all changed so much that I didn't really care to be around you, but I still missed you guys."

"Well, I'm glad you stayed strong," Alyssa said. "If you had given into everything that we gave into, then I don't think our lives would be as good as they are now."

"Yeah!" Marielle exclaimed as she pulled her hair into a ponytail. "And we wouldn't have become friends."

"We were all so eager to party with Chris and his older cousins that we never stopped to think about the consequences," Alyssa said. "You were the only one who didn't give in. You are such a good influence on people, Chantal. And that fact that you are still able to function while your boyfriend is in a coma demonstrates how real your faith is. I mean, look at how messed up Lisa, Bobby, Jason, and Cathy are about Andy. Lisa is smoking more weed than Cathy now; Bobby is struggling with football; Jason is drowning his sorrow in booze; and Cathy is, basically, unrecognizable. Yet, you are the closest with Andy, and you're stable. It's amazing."

Marielle nodded in agreement. "The way you have reacted to everything is one of the biggest reasons why I want a relationship with God," she admitted. "I don't understand it, but I want to."

Chantal's face had nearly turned as red as her auburn hair. "Thanks, guys," she said. "I'm really blessed."

Later that day after church, Jessie went into the church's bookstore. She rarely shopped there because her father had an entire library of Christian doctrine, music, and movies in their home. Jessie walked into the store without knowing what she was looking for, but all the while knowing that there was something she needed to buy. It was one of the strange things that sometimes happened to her, and she had learned not to question the urge when it came upon her. She believed it was the Holy Spirit tugging on her heart.

The store grew crowded as Jessie looked around, wondering what she was supposed to purchase. None of the books caught her eye, nor did any of the jewelry. She contemplated buying a new Bible case, but decided it was unnecessary. Turning away from the Bible cases, she came face to face with a rack of CDs. Her heart began pounding heavily against her chest as her blue eyes locked onto Switchfoot's *A Beautiful Letdown. I have this whole album on iTunes*, she thought. Picking it up off of the shelf, she turned away from the rack and began reading its case. Her heart skipped a beat as she suddenly collided with someone.

"Oh! Excuse me!" she exclaimed, tearing her eyes off of the CD and placing them onto the boy she had walked into.

Chris Dunkin stared back at her with sparkling eyes and a friendly smile. "It's okay, Jessie," he said and took a step back to let her pass by.

"Thanks," Jessie replied, smiling slightly as she walked past him. He had been standing near the Bibles with his girlfriend Marielle. Jessie recognized Marielle from her French class.

Recently, Jessie had noticed more and more MLH students coming to church. Chantal Kagelli had always attended, but then came Courtney Angeletti, then Chris Dunkin, and now, Marielle Kayne. While singing during the service, Jessie thought she even saw Alyssa Kelly and Jon Anderson in the crowd. It was an awesome, yet extremely surprising sight to see.

Although Jessie had never been one to care about popularity, she was not blind to the existence of it. Any boy who hung out with Chris and Jason was automatically "popular." Chris and Jason had the connections with the upper classmen; they knew where all the "cool" parties were; they knew how to capture everyone's attention. The girls that Chris, Jason, and their friends chose to date automatically became "popular." Pathetically, that was the way their class' social system had been functioning since seventh grade. When the three Montgomery middle schools combined for high school, a secondary popular group had formed, which only brought more drama to their already shallow social system. That's where Andy, Lisa, and "that crew" came into play. They were student council members, cheerleaders, and jocks. The majority of Jessie's grade viewed Andy's crew as the "good" popular group and Jason's crew as the "bad" popular group.

It had amazed Jessie to see the darkest member the "bad" group, Chris, come so radically to the light. *I wish I knew him*, she thought as she walked through the store. *I want to know how he ended up in church!* When Chris became a Christian two months prior, he threw their entire grade for a loop. It had caused an undeniable divide that tore apart the most intimidating clique in the freshmen halls. With Chris and Jason heading in opposite directions, their friends feeling torn in half, and no one knowing what to make

55

of it, pinpointing the "popular" clique became impossible. As a result, MLH had become a much more comfortable environment for the freshmen class. *I cannot believe how much good is coming from Chris's newfound faith,* she thought as she glanced back at him. *Clearly, he is sincere.*

The next thing Jessie knew, she was at the register purchasing a CD that she already owned. It made no sense, yet that was nothing new. She had learned a long time ago that God's ways did not always seem sensible. After leaving the bookstore, Jessie spotted her father in the corridor.

"Doing some shopping?" her father asked with a smile as she approached him.

"Strangely," Jessie replied and stopped at her father's side.

"Pastor Mark!" a voice suddenly called out. Jessie and her father turned around to see Chris and Marielle walking toward them.

"Hey, Chris," Jessie's father greeted him. Once Chris caught up to them, Jessie's father firmly shook his hand.

"This is my girlfriend, Marielle, who I told you about," Chris said.

"Hi, Marielle," Jessie's father said with a warm smile. "What did you think of the service?"

"I thought it was interesting," Marielle replied. "It was not scary at all. For some reason, I was nervous that it would be. I'm glad I came today."

"Good," Jessie's father said. "Do you two know my daughter, Jessie?"

"You're in my French class, right?" Marielle asked in a friendly tone.

"Yeah, with Ms. Gagnon," Jessie replied.

"Cool. Now I have someone to talk to," Marielle said. "I don't know anyone in our class, so I always just sit in the back."

"And we kind of know each other, right Jessie?" Chris joked. "We've bumped into each other here and there."

"Literally," Jessie said with a laugh. She felt her cheeks grow warm. "But, it's nice to finally get introduced to you. I was at your game Friday night. You played really well."

56

Chris raised his eyebrows. "Oh wow, you came to the game?" he said with wide eyes. "That's awesome! Thanks!"

"Yeah, it was fun," Jessie replied, feeling oddly at ease with Chris. He seemed to genuinely appreciate her support. Everything about him seemed sincere.

"Do you guys want to go out for breakfast?" Chantal Kagelli asked as she appeared between Marielle and Chris. "My parents just offered to take us. Oh, hi, Pastor Mark. Hi, Jessie!"

"I'm up for whatever she's up for," Chris replied and nodded toward Marielle.

"That was nice of them," Marielle said. "I'm up for whatever."

"Do you want to come with us?" Chantal asked Jessie.

"Oh...ummm," Jessie stammered, completely thrown off by Chantal's invitation. Although she knew Chantal from youth group, they had not hung out since seventh grade.

"You should come with us," Marielle chimed in. "We can speak in French and pretend we know what we're talking about," she joked.

Jessie smiled slightly. "Can I go, Dad?" she asked hesitantly and glanced up at her father.

"I don't see why not," he agreed.

Fifteen minutes later, Jessie was sandwiched between Alyssa and Marielle in Mrs. Kagelli's car. Mr. Kagelli was driving in front of them with Chris and Jon. *I cannot believe I am in a car with Jason's friends,* Jessie thought. *God, what door are you opening for me?*

Chapter 13

Sunday afternoon, Jason was sitting at his computer and chatting online. He was still feeling under the weather and still sporting sweatpants and a t-shirt. His mother had offered to take him to the doctor's, saying that he could have the flu. Jason had assured her that was not the case, so she finally left him alone with a bottle of water, homemade chicken soup, and an orange.

Chris popped up on chat shortly after two o'clock. *Well, here goes nothing,* Jason thought as he began typing…

Jason: yo, u there dude?

Chris: hey what's up?

Jason: nothing, kinda sick… what did u do today?

Chris: I just got home from church & breakfast

Jason: Oh ic

Chris: so what's up?

Jason: Nothing, had a rough weekend… still recovering

Chris: you went out with Luke right?

Jason: Yeah… I don't even want to talk about it

Chris: that bad?

Jason: You have no idea

Chris: I thought u were trying to keep away from that kinda stuff

Jason: Yeah I know, I know… I learned a good lesson, trust me. I woke up next to Cathy Saturday morning… evidently Luke called her to come take care of me

Chris: You're a mess

Jason: Tomorrow's gonna be interesting at school… she's probably going to punch me. I woke up and left without even saying bye. I couldn't dude. I need to stay away from her.

Chris: yeah you do. Marc told me he hooked up with Julianna

Jason: Oh wonderful, another connection for Cathy to my brothers' crew… she'll use that to her advantage. Hey so I've been thinking… I want to start volunteering somewhere. Like for some charity or something. Any ideas?

Chris: woah wicked random. where did that come from?

Jason: I don't know, I just think it's the right thing to do. I've wasted too much time doing bad things. I'd like to make up for some of them. If that's even possible.

Chris: Um, are you okay?

Jason: LOL yeah I'm serious though… if you can think of anything at your church, or like if you hear of something going on at school, let me know.

Chris: okay dude, that's pretty cool. You'd come to my church?

Jason: Yeah

Chris: Did I miss something?

Jason: I told you man, I'm trying to straighten myself out. I haven't smoked weed in a week.

Chris: that's good… how about the Adderall?

Jason: Well, I still take it every day, but I stopped blowing it.

Chris: good. So what did you do, just drink too much at the party?

Jason: I was playing some drinking game with Matt and I downed like eleven beers in two hours… and evidently I had taken Vicodin with Sartelli earlier… I don't even remember. I got so sick… it was real bad.

Chris: I bet Matt was pretty mad

Jason: Yeah but he had some good advice for me. I guess it's good I messed up so bad. It kind of woke me up.

Chris: did you hear about a fight at my game? I heard Luke broke one up.

Jason: Oh that. You heard about that?

Chris: just that there was one. what happened?

Jason: O'Leary and his friends were being jerks. I had to straighten them out.

Chris: I figured you had something to do with it. Since when do you have a problem with Sean?

Jason: I don't but he was out of line… hitting on some girls

Chris: Like people we're friends with?

Jason: Nah, just some random girls

59

Chris: Since when do you care about random girls?

Jason: Well, these girls are good girls, you know, like people who should be respected.

Chris: interesting…

Jason: for whatever reason it just bothered me.

Chris: no offense dude but that's totally random. You're usually the one giving people a hard time

Jason: I don't want to get into it right now, but a few weeks back something caught my attention… and I don't know, it just changed something in me.

Chris: well that's good. I told you I'd help you out. Why don't you come talk to Pastor Mark with me on Wednesday?

Jason: I don't know… I'll think about it.

Chris: he's helped me out a lot. Do you know he sent his daughter to the game Friday just to cheer me on?

Jason: ic

Chris: she came out for breakfast with us today

Jason: are you serious?

Chris: yeah, why? do you know her?

Jason: yeah, but I never thought she'd want to hang out with people like us

Chris: LOL well Chantal's parents took us out for breakfast, she knows Chantal from church

Jason: yeah but that girl is like perfect, you and I have done so many crappy things… I'm surprised she'd give you the time of day… no offense

Chris: LOL her father gave both of us more than the time of day, so why wouldn't she?

Jason: I don't know, I guess in my mind she's just on a whole different level

Chris: don't look at it like that. She's definitely not judgmental. She sat there today and talked to Alyssa, Jon, and me like we had good reputations. I'm sure she knows some of the stuff I used to do, but she didn't look at me any differently than she looked at Chantal, who's wicked innocent

Jason: Yeah stuff you used to do, I still do

60

Chris: true but you're working on that. What I'm trying to say is that the people who go to my church are not perfect. Seriously, we all have pasts. Maybe Jessie and Chantal are innocent, but they're a minority. Most people are like you and me. They have screwed up a lot. I think we appreciate it even more, because we've been forgiven for so much.

Jason: Church people seem untouchable to me… you keep it real, but that's cause you're my boy. I don't know why Pastor Mark took an interest in either of us, but that's rare. I'd be surprised if another Christian even looked my way. Why would God have an interest in me?

Chris: I've done worse things than you, and God has helped me. Maybe volunteering will help you realize that you can bring some good to this world.

Jason: I'd like to do that… I liked planning that service for Andy.

Chris: why don't you come talk to Pastor Mark with me? God can help you way more than anyone else. You need to repent and accept Jesus as your Savior. God favors no one. He will do for you what He has done for me.

Jason: I'll think about it… really, I will.

Chris: all right, I'm praying for you.

Jason: thanks bro

Chris: see ya tomorrow in homeroom

Jason: k peace

Chris: later

Chapter 14

Monday morning, Cathy Kagelli walked into homeroom right as the bell was ringing. Each second in the same room with Chantal, Alyssa, and Marielle was about as pleasant to Cathy as having a tooth pulled. She slumped into her assigned seat beside Chantal and turned away from her.

"Hey, so is Jay scared that O'Leary is going to come after him?" a boy, who seemed to suddenly appear at Cathy's desk, asked her.

"Excuse me?" Cathy retorted and shot an annoyed glare in his direction.

"Friday night, you know, the fight they got in," the boy replied as if it were common sense.

"What fight?!" Cathy exclaimed. *Why does some random boy think he knows more about Jason than I do?*

"At the game, O'Leary and his friends were talking to some girls, and Jason came out of nowhere and sucker-punched him," the boy said. "Isn't he your boyfriend?"

"What girls?" Cathy questioned him and shook her head in confusion. "Jason has no issue with Sean. I was with Jason after the game, and he said nothing about a fight. Maybe you shouldn't listen to every rumor you hear."

The boy laughed. "I didn't hear about it! I was there for it," he stated.

Cathy squinted. "Are you serious?" she asked, carefully changing her tone from pretentious to curious.

"Wow, I can't believe he didn't tell you. Maybe he didn't want to get you mad," the boy said. "Most girls don't like hearing about fights."

"Well, I want to know about *this* fight," Cathy stated impatiently. "What girls was Sean talking to? Were they my friends?"

"No," the boy said and shook his head, "*definitely not.* I think your sister knows them. Chantal, who are those girls that sit up front in our English class?" he asked.

"What?" Chantal asked and glanced up at him. "English class? Oh, Jessie and Sarah?"

"Yeah...yeah!" the boy exclaimed and snapped his fingers. "Jessie Robins and Sarah Gleeson."

Cathy dropped her jaw. "What?!" she cried out in disbelief. "Jason got in a fight with Sean O'Leary over some choir princess? Jason and I don't pay attention to people like that. He must have some other issue with Sean."

"Jason did *what*?" Chantal asked.

"Well, it looked that way to me," the boy stated and glanced from Cathy to Chantal. "I thought it was pretty cool of him. Those girls are nice. O'Leary can be a tool sometimes."

Cathy lowered her eyebrows in disgust and flipped her hair over her shoulder. "Jason was probably just drunk," she mumbled as she placed her arms across her chest and rolled her eyes.

On his way to second period, Jason stopped to get a book from his locker. As he opened the narrow aluminum door, a folded piece of paper came flying out at him. Unlike most high school students, Jason kept his locker organized *at all times*. Papers did not typically fall out. Bending to the ground, Jason picked up the paper and began unfolding it. He immediately realized someone else's handwriting covered the sheet:

"Fumbling his confidence and wondering why the world has passed him by... Hoping that he's bent for more than arguments and failed attempts to fly... We were meant to live for so much more, have we lost ourselves? Somewhere we live inside... Somewhere we live inside... We were meant to live for so much more, have we lost ourselves? Somewhere we live inside... Dreaming about Providence and whether mice and men have second tries... Maybe we've been living with our eyes half open... Maybe we're bent and broken... broken... We want more than this world's got to offer... We want more than this world's got to offer... We want more than the wars of

our fathers… and everything inside <u>screams for second life</u>… Yeah, we were meant to live for so much more, have we lost ourselves?"[*]

Jason stared, dumbfounded, and read the quote over and over. *Who would give me something like this?* He wondered. Who could know the way he felt? He had only told Matt. *Matt would never go near the freshmen lockers.* Cathy did not even know about Jason's discontentment with life. No one knew.

The only person he could think to ask was Chris. He knew that the note was not written in Chris's handwriting, but thought Chris might recognize the quote. The fact that "second life" was underlined made Jason think it had something to do with God. It reminded him of something he had read in the Gospel of John on the night of Andy's prayer service. Strangely, no one knew that he had ever read the Gospel.

Folding the note into his cargo pocket, Jason headed to his AP Latin class. On the way, he ran into one of the last people he wanted to see: Sean O'Leary.

"Hey, Davids. Look, I'm sorry about Friday night, bro," Sean said as he approached Jason. "I was wasted. I never would have talked to that girl if I knew she was yours."

Surprised by Sean's words, Jason stared at him, speechlessly, for a moment.

"Tell Luke that I'm sorry, too," Sean added and extended his hand toward Jason.

Jason shook Sean's hand. "She's not my girlfriend," he said, "but she's someone I look out for. Just keep your friends away from her."

Sean nodded in recognition. Jason assumed that Sean was only showing him respect because he was Luke's younger brother. Anyone with a brain knew that messing with Jason meant messing with Luke, which inevitably meant messing with Matt. Considering

---

[*] *Lyrics from Switchfoot's "Meant to Live"*

the amount of respect that Matt had earned at MLH, even punks like Sean knew better than to antagonize him.

Jessie walked into her French class and took a seat toward the back of the room. Marielle was not there yet, and Jessie wondered if she would sit with her. At breakfast, Marielle had been friendly, but Jessie wasn't sure if that made them school-friends or not. Some girls would talk her ear off at church and then not even wave hello to her in school.

A few moments later, Marielle walked through the door, awkwardly juggling her binder, bookbag, and pocketbook. She plopped her binder down on the first vacant desk and then glanced around the room. When her eyes met with Jessie's, she smiled, picked up her binder, and walked toward the back of the room. Gracelessly dropping all of her stuff onto the desk beside Jessie, she let out a loud sigh. "I wish they let us go to our lockers more than three times a day!" she exclaimed and slumped into her seat. "I have too much stuff to carry everywhere."

Jessie smiled at Marielle. "How was the rest of your Sunday?"

"It was good," Marielle replied as she pulled her hair back into a ponytail. "Chris and I watched a movie with his little sister. Then we had dinner with his parents. It was really nice. What did you do?"

"My mom took me and Sarah out for dinner because my dad was working," Jessie said.

"Aw, that's nice!" Marielle cried. "I love going out to eat. Then again, I love food!"

Jessie laughed. "I'm with you on that."

"Breakfast was fun yesterday. Chris and I were really glad that you came," Marielle stated as she flipped open her book. "Chris said your dad's been a huge inspiration to him."

"Really?" Jessie asked. "I didn't even know they knew each other until my dad told me to go to Chris's game. It was fun cheering for him."

"Chris is awesome," Marielle said and smiled widely. "He amazes me in so many ways. It's probably good neither of us knew him before this year. We probably would not have liked him very much."

"Is he still friends with Jason Davids?" Jessie asked, hoping Marielle did not find her question odd.

"*Best* friends," Marielle replied with emphasis. "They don't hang out that much anymore, but Chris loves Jason. He said that Jason's been going through some stuff lately—trials are what Chris called them. I guess he even broke up with Cathy. I don't think people know that, so don't tell anyone. Jason doesn't want people bringing it up to her. I guess she's really upset about it."

Jessie's heart dropped to her stomach.

"I used to be afraid of Jason until Andy's prayer service," Marielle admitted, taking Jessie by surprise. "Jay actually talked to your dad for, like, an hour that day. I think their conversation had a big impact on him."

"Jason knows my dad?" Jessie asked—after picking her jaw up off of the floor. As she widened her eyes, she felt her face growing hot and most likely red.

"Wow, your dad keeps secrets well, huh?" Marielle laughed.

Jessie nodded. "So, you think my dad made an impact on him?" she asked.

Marielle nodded.

Jessie sat back in her seat and took a deep breath. It was only third period, and she already felt overwhelmed.

Chapter 15

Lisa Ankerman's green eyes protruded from her face as she stared at Cathy with a look of disbelief. "What?!" she exclaimed.

"Yeah, exactly," Cathy stated angrily and shook her head back and forth. "Why would he do that?"

Lisa lowered her eyebrows and stared at Cathy. The two girls were huddled over a table in the corner of the cafeteria, far from the rest of their friends. "Do you think that's why he wants space from you?" Lisa questioned Cathy and raised her eyebrows. "Could he have some interest in this church-girl?"

Cathy felt her eyes fill with tears at the sound of Lisa's words.

"I don't mean to upset you," Lisa said as her normally cold eyes filled with compassion. "I just think there is something we could do if that's the case."

"What?" Cathy asked and wiped the corner of her eyes.

"What we do best—raise hell," Lisa said and smiled sweetly.

Jessie watched as Leslie Lucus entered their seventh period Algebra class. Instead of taking her usual seat on the left side of the classroom, Leslie trucked over to the far-right corner. Jumping into the seat beside Jessie, Leslie turned to her and smiled widely. "Hi, Jessie!" she exclaimed.

Startled by Leslie's friendliness, Jessie eyed Leslie warily. "Hi," she replied quietly.

"It was nice running into you after the game on Friday night," Leslie said and widened her bright green eyes. "Did you and your friend have fun?"

"Ye-ah," Jessie said gradually, wondering why Leslie was talking to her.

"It was a great game!" Leslie cried. "I love cheering for Chris. He is *such* a good running back. Do you know him?"

"Not really," Jessie replied and stared skeptically at Leslie.

"Oh, he is one of my *favorite* people," Leslie stressed enthusiastically. "That's so cool how he is, like, all about church now! I heard that he goes *every* week. Is that true?"

Jessie eyed Leslie cautiously, trying to figure out her motives. Leslie, unlike her friends, was friendly to people outside of her clique. She was also known for being two-faced. Jessie had always assumed that Leslie talked to people just to find out information so that her friends could gossip.

"I don't know. I don't really know him," Jessie replied and turned around to face the front of the classroom.

"But, isn't your dad his pastor?" Leslie asked and leaned in toward Jessie's desk. "Your dad did a *really* good job at Andy's prayer service, and you did *such* a good job singing. Ah, seriously, hearing you sing made me cry! You have such talent!"

Jessie turned to face Leslie, smiled slightly, and then turned immediately back around. "Thanks," she added, while peering straight ahead.

"I had never seen you at a football game before," Leslie continued, seeming to disregard Jessie's standoffish behavior. "What made you come? You should come to more! The team loves the support."

Jessie did not want to be rude and tell Leslie to stop talking to her, but she realized that Leslie was trying to pump her for information. Although, she could not figure out why. "My youth group was cancelled," Jessie answered flatly.

"Ohhhh, youth group!" Leslie cried and smiled sweetly. "That's really cute. Does Chris go to that when he doesn't have a game?"

Jessie turned and looked Leslie directly in the eye. "Why are you asking me all these questions, Leslie?" she asked. "I already told you that I don't know Chris. What are you trying to find out?"

Leslie's demeanor did not waver. "Nothing," she replied, appearing undisturbed by Jessie's bold remark. "I just hope you come to more games! You seem like a really nice person, and I would love to hang out with you sometime."

Jessie widened her eyes and stared at Leslie in disbelief. She had no interest in hanging out with Leslie, but at the same time, she wanted to be kind. "That's nice of you to say," Jessie said politely.

Jessie believed that she had the gift of spiritual discernment. She could sense when someone was dishonest or had manipulative intentions. She also believed strongly in spiritual warfare, realizing that there was an ongoing battle surrounding each human daily. If God was drawing her to Jason and doing some work in his life, she knew both of them were in for a battle. The last thing Satan wanted was for Jason to put his faith in Christ. Satan was going to do everything in his power to torment Jason and attack anyone God was working through to reach Jason. Although spiritual warfare sounded scary, Jessie knew that Satan could not do anything to her—or any other Christians—without first getting God's permission. If God allowed Satan to tempt or attack her, then He would work it together for good. Leslie's strange behavior made Jessie realize that the battle had begun, and that she needed to begin praying fervently for Jason's salvation.

"Hey, so what's this I hear about you digging a choir-girl?" Jeff Brooke asked Jason during eighth period. "What's that about?"

"What dude?!" Jason exclaimed with a short laugh.

"Yeah, at the game Friday night, you fought Sean O'Leary over some church-girl," Jeff stated with an amused smile. "At least that's what's going around."

"Going around where? I haven't heard that," Jason said and rolled his eyes.

"That's what Cathy heard, and she's pretty upset, dude," Jeff replied.

"She needs to not worry about rumors," Jason said nonchalantly. "She knows where we stand."

"So, it didn't happen?" Jeff asked.

"I didn't say *that*," Jason said and widened his bright blue eyes. "But she shouldn't get upset over me being nice to people. It just shows you how ridiculous she can be."

Jeff laughed. "Well, she's *Cathy Kagelli*! What can you expect?"

Jason rolled his eyes.

"So, that girl isn't anything to you?" Jeff asked.

"A girl like that could never be anything to me," Jason stated flatly.

"Isn't that kind of harsh?" Jeff asked, clearly mistaking Jason's intent.

"No, dude. She just stays away from people like me," Jason said with a shrug. "She's smart," he laughed, "it's no secret that I'm screwed up."

"So, you don't like her?" Jeff asked.

"Did your girlfriend put you up to this?" Jason questioned him. "I know Lisa is Cathy's partner in crime."

"That, she is," Jeff agreed. "But no, I just wanted to find out the facts for myself. Before rumors start flying around this place, I'd like to know my rights from my lefts."

"O'Leary and I squared everything away, so there's no need for any talk to fly around," Jason said. "Neither one of us wants to hear about Friday night. What's done is done. We were both drunken idiots."

Chapter 16

Since September, Matt had been driving Jason to school. Even though Matt was a partier by reputation, he was a good influence on Jason. Tuesday morning, Luke offered to drive Jason to school. Seeing that Luke rarely offered, Jason took him up on it.

"So, we're just going to make a little pit stop on the way," Luke said as he pulled his BMW out of their street.

"What are you talking about?" Jason asked.

"Don't worry, little bro. I have you covered," Luke said and laughed.

"Where are we going?" Jason questioned him, suddenly wishing that he had left with Matt.

"This is a 'Luke Davids Special,'" Luke stated and put on a pair of sunglasses.

"Luke, I have a test this morning!" Jason cried out in protest. "I have a Latin test, second period."

"Oooh, that's cutting it close," Luke sang and shook his head. "Hopefully, I'll have you back by then."

"You are unbelievable," Jason said and sighed. "Just let me out right here. I'll walk to school."

"Calm down, you've already been excused from class," Luke stated matter-of-factly.

"What are you talking about?" Jason asked, while eyeing his brother warily.

"I have ways," Luke replied mysteriously. "Here, take one of these; it will help you relax." He laughed and tossed Jason a bottle of No-Doz.

"Oh yeah, good idea! Pump me with caffeine!" Jason cried in annoyance.

"Um, yeah…you won't find much caffeine in there," Luke said dryly as he turned up his stereo.

Jason popped open the bottle of pills and poured a few into his hand. They were small, unmarked and white. "This looks like aspirin," Jason commented as he flipped one over. Studying it closely, he noticed a smiley face was embossed on one side. Jason

71

jumped in his seat. He quickly threw the pills back in the bottle. "Get these things away from me!" he exclaimed and threw the bottle at his brother.

"You told me you wanted to roll," Luke said. "Today's the perfect opportunity. Mom called us both out for the day. Well, by 'Mom' I mean Missy's older sister. There's a whole crew ready."

"Dude, I am *not* taking ecstasy!" Jason stated firmly, feeling a sudden sense of anxiety come over him. "You have lost your mind."

"Um, what?" Luke asked with a laugh.

"Do I need to call Matt and have him come get me?" Jason threatened Luke, knowing that Matt would freak out on him.

"You're the one who asked me for these!" Luke exclaimed and shook his head.

"What are you talking about?!" Jason cried out in defense. "I've never taken ecstasy! I'm not going to *add* to the list of drugs I've tried."

"Friday night, you asked if you could roll," Luke said, "and I said *no way*. Then I thought about it and figured you'd just try it with your friends. If you're going to do it, I'd rather it be with me."

"Friday night, I almost got my stomach pumped. Do you think I actually remember saying that?" Jason asked, feeling instantly disgusted with himself.

"What happened to you?" Luke questioned him. "You're usually begging me to get you pills."

"Yeah, and you don't need to remind me of that," Jason said. He felt completely disgusted with himself *and* his brother. Why was it so hard for him to stay away from drugs? Did everyone get offered ecstasy at seven in the morning? Why wouldn't temptation leave him alone? Of course, Jason wanted to try it. Of course, he wanted to know what Luke's friends raved about. Jason knew that ecstasy would provide a temporary escape from his problems, but then leave him feeling worse off, emotionally and physically.

"Fine. We'll go out for breakfast, and then I'll drop you off at school," Luke said calmly. "Don't get so mad. I thought I was doing you a favor."

"Just have me there by eight-thirty," Jason stated, leaning his head back and closing his eyes. It had taken every ounce of strength he had to turn down Luke's offer. *How does Chris stay away from this crap?*

Jessie walked into homeroom and felt twenty pairs of eyes lock on her while she took her seat. The hairs on her arms stood up straight and a chill shot up her spine.

"Jessie," Katherine Rossi called softly from two seats away, "if you feel like everyone's staring at you, it's only because people heard about the fight between Jason and Sean." She got up and knelt by Jessie's desk. "Don't let it get to you," she said and smiled sympathetically. "I just want you to know that I don't agree with what my friends are doing."

Jessie eyed Katherine in confusion, wondering what she was talking about, and why she was being nice. Jessie did not pick up on any insincerity in Katherine and felt badly for assuming that she was a snob. "Thanks," Jessie replied and smiled slightly.

"I'm sure Jason will put Cathy in her place," Katherine whispered. "Jon said that you hung out with him and everyone after church. That's really good because none of them will let this get far. They're good people."

Jessie nodded, wondering exactly what people were saying about her and Jason.

Chantal Kagelli sat in homeroom, resting her head in her hands. She was praying silently for the strength to restrain herself from slamming Cathy's face into the desk. It had only been twenty-four hours since Cathy had found out about Jason's fight; yet, somehow, slanderous rumors were already flying around their school. A senior had mistaken Chantal for Cathy before homeroom and asked her if she was going to *fight* Jessie! Chantal could not believe that Cathy was cruel enough to pull Jessie into her drama with Jason.

Cathy had made it sound like she and Jason were still together so that she looked like a victim, Jason looked like a cheater, and Jessie looked like a whore. Of course, the rumors hadn't stopped

73

with Jason *liking* Jessie; they went as far as insinuating a hidden relationship between them. How could the rumors have gotten so undeniably out of hand in just one day?

Chapter 17

Jason eyed his brother suspiciously as they sat inside a diner one town over from Montgomery. Luke certainly had done a good job gathering a crowd for the occasion. Jason could not believe that everyone sitting around the table was planning to roll, day and night, at a club in Springfield. Luke had even found Jason a fake ID. How he had kept Matt from hearing about his plan was mind-boggling.

"Are you sure you want to go to school today?" Marc Dunkin asked and stared at Jason expectantly.

"Are you sure you *don't* want to go to school today, Marc?" Jason retorted. "When Matt finds out about this you better be ready to kiss his butt. The last thing he needs is you benched for the playoffs."

"I'm not an idiot," Marc said flatly. "Seniors are allowed to sign themselves out of school, and playoffs or not, drugs aren't my thing. Red Bull will keep me going all day. You could come and just drink that, you know."

Jason lowered his eyebrows and considered his options. The thought of going to a rave without taking drugs had never occurred to him.

"You and Cathy are broken up, so you could at least come for the girls," Marc added.

"Don't put me on the spot like that, dude," Jason laughed. He looked up at the ceiling and shook his head.

"Jay's made his decision," Luke said with a smirk. "He's not game for a Tuesday-afternoon rave. Then again, he's only fifteen."

Jason widened his eyes angrily. Luke knew that Jason hated being put down because of his age. Whenever Luke teased him about it, Jason would cave into pressure, always feeling the need to prove himself. That was exactly what had happened at Samson's party. After being sick all weekend, Jason had decided to swallow his pride the next time Luke challenged him. As Jason stared intensely at Luke, he felt his pride sliding down his throat. "Matt's eighteen, and he wouldn't be up for it either," Jason retorted. "So don't even try to play the age card."

Luke raised his eyebrows and glanced around the large table, appearing speechless.

"He's right," Marc stated with a nod. "Matt's going to kick your #$%," he added and slapped Luke playfully in the shoulder.

***

Jason arrived at school ten minutes before second period. He had never felt so proud of himself. "I passed up ecstasy for a Latin exam," he said quietly as he headed to his locker. "That is *awesome!*"

Jason hesitated slightly before opening his locker, wondering if he would find another mystery note. He still had the other one in his backpack and was planning to show it to Chris at lunch. As Jason pulled his locker open, a smile spread across his face. Sure enough, a note had fallen to his feet. Unfolding the paper, Jason recognized the same handwriting that had covered the first note.

"Yesterday is a wrinkle on your forehead... yesterday is a promise that you've broken... don't close your eyes, don't close your eyes... this is your life and today is all you've got now, and today is all you'll ever have... don't close your eyes, don't close your eyes... this is your life, are you who you want to be? This is your life, are you who you want to be? This is your life, is it everything you dreamed that it would be, when the world was younger and you had everything to lose?"*

Jason read the note, wondering who would write such stirring words. Whoever it was knew him well and knew how to entice him. There was no way that Cathy would leave him with such encouraging words, nor would any of her friends. Jason thought of Chantal, wondering if she knew anything about his situation. Jason doubted that Cathy had confided much in Chantal. Cathy could not understand Chantal and hated the way she outshined her. Thinking

---

* Lyrics from Switchfoot's "This is Your Life"

of that brought Jason back to something he had once read. "The light shined in the darkness, and the darkness did not comprehend it," he recited slowly to himself. "Wow, that's pretty true."

After folding the note into his pocket, Jason grabbed his Latin binder and closed his locker. He was halfway to his classroom when the bell rang. Immediately, the corridor flooded with people. Strangely, Jason did not have the urge to trip anyone or call anyone fat; he felt like being *nice.*

He felt different inside, but he could not figure out why everyone else seemed to know. Everyone he walked past stared at him; some people looked scared and others looked upset. Normally, he would have confronted them all, but today, he felt like being a decent person.

"Yo, Jay!" Chris cried out and grabbed ahold of Jason's backpack, yanking him aside.

"Woah, what's up dude?" Jason asked and stared at Chris warily.

"Where have you been?" Chris questioned him, while eyeing him intently.

Jason rolled his eyes. "Long story, but you'll be really proud of me when I tell you. I have a test in a few minutes though, so I have to boot. What's going on?"

Chris swallowed deeply. "I don't know dude, but hell broke loose this morning, and everyone's talking a lot of crap about you and Pastor Mark's daughter," he stated quickly.

"What?!" Jason exclaimed, completely caught off guard by Chris's words. "What do you mean people are talking crap? I'll kill them."

Chris nodded. "Yeah, you really need to do something. I feel so bad for Jessie; she looked pretty upset when I saw her."

Jason's eyes grew wide. "What do you mean?" he asked, wondering if he looked as concerned as he felt.

Chris sighed. "I don't know who started anything, but it's going around that you cheated on Cathy with Jessie. People are saying that you and Cathy never broke up, and that you and Jessie had a secret relationship. People think that's why you punched Sean the other night. It's a mess. I mean, it's all I've heard anyone talk about since I got here."

Jason blinked his eyes and stared speechlessly at Chris. He opened his mouth to speak, paused for a few seconds, and then shut it. He shook his head from side to side and placed his arms across his chest. "I'm going to kill her," he said after a moment.

"You need to tell me, so I can get your back, how do you and Jessie know each other?" Chris demanded sternly.

"We don't!" Jason cried earnestly and widened his eyes. "I saw Sean hitting on her, and it made me *really* mad. Her dad was so nice to me. I couldn't watch someone try to take advantage of her. They kept telling Sean to leave them alone, and he wouldn't. He had a few friends with him, and it was just a bad situation. I wouldn't take that punch back for anything."

"When I asked you about the fight, why didn't you tell me it was about Jessie?" Chris questioned him.

Jason dropped his eyes to the floor and stood in silence for a moment. "I didn't want any praise for it, and I didn't want to draw attention to her," he said hesitantly as he glanced up at Chris.

"Why?" Chris asked, flaring his arms out and squinting in confusion.

Of course, he's confused. He knows me, Jason thought. He shook his head and dropped his arms to his sides. He bit his bottom lip and stared blankly at the floor for a moment. "Because I care," he admitted quietly and shrugged. "I have to go, guy. I have a test to ace." Without waiting for Chris's reaction, Jason hustled off toward his classroom.

Chapter 18

The moment Jason passed in his Latin exam, he asked his teacher for a pass to the bathroom. To his surprise, no one in class had said anything to him about Jessie, Cathy, or the fight. He realized that he intimidated most people—because he had no problem being offensive—and that Jessie was an innocent, unthreatening, easy target for gossip's cruel attack. Whoever had started the rumor was naïve to think that Jason would not defend Jessie. After all, he had punched someone because of her.

Having dated Cathy for two years, Jason was familiar with her manipulative tactics. He assumed that she was mad at him for leaving Samson's and jealous that he had defended another girl. *What a perfect motive for creating such an awful rumor,* Jason thought. It was to Cathy's advantage that Jason had not told many people about their break. He had done that out of respect for Cathy's feelings, and he could not believe how quickly she had taken advantage of his gesture.

If this didn't originate with Cathy then it came from Lisa or Leslie, Jason reasoned. *That would explain why Jeff had asked so many questions about Jessie.* It really did not matter to Jason whose idea it had been; he knew, without a doubt, that they were all guilty. No one ever wanted to cross Cathy because everyone knew she had an army behind her, always ready to attack.

Although Jason thought Lisa was cool, he knew she was just as ruthless as Cathy. Lisa's flawless beauty intimidated people, and she used it as a weapon. Her sarcastic attitude added the finishing touch, along with her student council position and sibling-like friendship with Andy. *Anyone who can pull off being best friends with Andy Rosetti and Cathy Kagelli knows how to charm a crowd.* Lisa was Cathy's sharpest weapon.

Leslie was Cathy's second sharpest weapon. She was a blonde-haired, bright-eyed, Marcia-Brady-gone-evil nightmare. The majority of their class thought that Leslie was the female version of Andy—perfect in every way. No one ever expected her to speak a harsh word or do anything inhumane. Jason considered Leslie an even more dangerous weapon than Lisa because no one realized that she was one.

Cathy also had servants—like Julianna—who based their lives around pleasing her. Jason realized that he had also played right into Cathy's chain of command for almost two years. She had used him as a servant and as a weapon since the day they had begun dating. *How did I not see it?*

Making his way through the vacant corridor, Jason sought out Cathy's classroom. He walked past the doorway three times before she came out of the room. For the first time, Cathy did not look attractive. Even though he realized that she had a right to be mad at him, he hated her for tormenting someone as innocent as Jessie.

"You need to listen to me, right *now*," Jason stated angrily and grabbed ahold of Cathy's arm, yanking her into the nearby boy's bathroom. He locked the door and pinned her against the wall. "If I find out that you had *anything* to do with these rumors flying around, I promise you that we are done forever."

Cathy attempted to push Jason off of her, but he held her firmly against the wall.

"Tell me why people think I cheated on you!" Jason demanded.

"Tell me why you did," Cathy replied and glared at him.

"I'm not going to believe for a second that you think I cheated on you with that innocent girl," Jason stated while stepping back from Cathy and throwing his arms up in the air. "You know why I need space from you. You know how much I love you. You know I would never cheat on you."

"So, you didn't?" Cathy asked and flashed her bright white, sweet smile.

Jason stared at her in disbelief. "I cannot believe you are playing this card right now! Cathy, I *know* you started the rumors. Don't kid yourself. No one in his right mind would come against me like this. I am *sorry* about what happened Friday night. I am *sorry* that Luke invited you over and that I woke up not knowing why you were next to me. I'm *sorry* that I left without saying goodbye, but I had to! I need space right now. You can hate me all you want and try to ruin my already *horrible* reputation until you turn blue in the face. I don't care! What I want to know is why you think it's OK to hurt innocent people, every day of your life?"

Cathy let out a short laugh and rolled her eyes. "Oh, come on, you do the exact same thing! Don't you think it hurts people's feelings when you call them losers, fat, dorks, or ugly? You hurt people all the time! That's why everyone is afraid of you!" she exclaimed and placed her arms across her chest.

"Teasing people to their faces is a lot different than making up lies behind their backs," Jason stated angrily. "Because of you, Jon thought Chantal hated him for over a year—not to mention Chantal was devastated over their breakup! Then you stole her best friend. You torment your own flesh and blood because you thrive off the power it gives you. The second you have a reason to be jealous of someone, you set out to destroy them. That's why you hate Courtney Angeletti, and I know that's why you're so mean to Chantal. So, let me guess? When you heard that I stood up for Jessie at the football game you got jealous? Why do I think that? Because someone is trying to ruin her reputation, and the only person psychotic enough to do that is you!"

Cathy stared at Jason with a look of wide-eyed disbelief.

"I want you to do everything in your power to quench these rumors," Jason stated, trying to calm down. "Evidently, people think that I have a 'secret' relationship with Jessie and that she wronged you. I don't even know her. I know her father. He helped me a lot with Andy's prayer service. I owed him one, OK? When I saw Sean harassing Jessie, I jumped in out of respect for her father. You know that I love you, but if you don't apologize to Jessie, I will have no problem forgetting we ever dated." *Ouch. Okay, Jason, you could have been a little nicer or maybe held back that last sentence. She's going to kill you.*

"Wow, you really think I want us to get back together, huh?" Cathy shot back and shook her head. "I don't care if you forget that we ever dated! I also did not make up these wonderful rumors. I wish I was that clever."

But you are that clever. "Well, I'm so glad that we have this all straightened out," Jason said with a smirk. "I don't have to worry about your feelings anymore, nor do I have to defend your reputation. Seeing how ridiculous you are, that had become a full-time job for me! Now I can put my energy toward getting Lisa and Leslie kicked off cheerleading because if *you* didn't make up the rumors, then they did. I'm sure I can get Matt's girlfriend to reevaluate their abilities."

"Jason, once a rumor starts spreading it takes a lot more than an apology to put a stop to it," Cathy retorted. "If anyone can make it stop, it's you. You're the only person I know—besides your brothers—with enough power to do it. Good luck with that. My damage has already been done." She shrugged carelessly, unlocked the door, and breezed out of the bathroom. Jason stared blankly at the closing door, wondering how he had been blind to her callous behavior for so long.

Chapter 19

It certainly was bizarre, walking through the halls of her high school and hearing her name rattle off everyone's tongue. Instead of defending herself, Jessie sat during second period *praising* God for her situation. She believed two important things: the trial was part of God's perfect plan for her life, and for Satan to be attacking her so badly, she must be doing something right. *Satan attacks people who are a threat to him,* Jessie reminded herself. *Thank God, I know that attacks only test my faith and strengthen my character. God will never give me more than I can handle.*

This battle is a spiritual matter—a battle over Jason's soul. She thought of the Apostle Paul's words to the Ephesians, *"Put on the whole armor of God, that you may be able to stand against the wiles of the devil. For we do not wrestle against flesh and blood, but against principalities, against powers, against the rulers of darkness of this age, against spiritual hosts of wickedness in heavenly places."*

Unfortunately for Satan, the ultimate battle had already been won. When Jesus died on the cross and rose from the dead, He defeated death and opened the gates of heaven for all those who believe in Him. What happened on the Cross—two thousand years ago—made Jessie understand how ignorant Satan was in comparison to God. Satan had possessed Judas to betray Jesus, which led to Jesus' crucifixion. All along, Satan thought that he was winning the battle, having the Son of God brutally murdered. As a result of that murder, death was defeated, and sinners were able to enter into the Kingdom of Heaven by believing that Jesus—the Messiah—paid their sins' penalty on the Cross. When Jesus rose from the dead, Satan ultimately lost. What Satan had meant for evil, God had intended for good.

Jessie knew that Satan was the prince of deception, that all lies came from him, and that he was incapable of speaking the truth without twisting it. *What is going on around me? A bunch of lies are circulating about the boy God is drawing me toward and me. A coincidence? Nope,* Jessie reasoned. *There is no such thing as a coincidence, only God working things together for His purpose.*

It did not matter to Jessie what people thought of her. She was thankful to have been brought up relying on God for strength; He had never failed her. Although she wondered if Jason would stick up for her, she did not waste her time worrying over it. God had His hand in everything from the start. She knew that she was in His will, and she was not about to back down in fear of evil lies.

Entering his third period History class, Jason dropped his book on the desk beside Bryan and immediately stalked across the room to Julianna Camen. Julianna lifted her eyes from her paper and glanced at Jason in a frightful manner. He hopped onto the vacant desk in front of her and spun around so that he was directly in her face.

Julianna swallowed and raised her eyebrows. She took a deep breath and cocked her head to the side.

I can't believe how nervous I make this girl, Jason thought. "So, Julianna, how's your day going?" he asked and smiled at her.

"Fine…I guess," she replied hesitantly.

"Did you have fun at the party the other night? I saw you sleeping with Marc when I left. It *looked* like you had a good time," Jason said with a laugh.

Julianna's face grew red as she dropped her eyes to her desk.

Jason leaned in closer and brought his voice down to a whisper. "I don't really want to harass you about Marc Dunkin. I don't care if you turn yourself into one of his many whores. I just want to give you a little warning. It's not worth becoming a mean person just to fit in with people like Cathy and Lisa. You're just going to hate yourself for it in the long run, and they'll hate you in due time, anyway. It's the way the system works. Nice talk, Julianna," Jason said and knocked on her desk as he jumped up. "And don't spread rumors; they'll come back to haunt you," he added before heading across the room to his seat.

Chapter 20

Later that morning, Jason entered the Blue House in his high school, where the senior classrooms were located. He had ten minutes to find Matt and make it to Geometry. Luckily, Matt was an easy person to spot, being over six feet tall and often surrounded by a group of football players.

As Jason hustled through the senior halls, he thought about Cathy and her audacity. He could finally see the ugliness in Cathy that his friends had warned him about. He could not understand what he had seen in her for so long. She had mesmerized him, making him blind to the destruction that she continuously caused. Suddenly, everything seemed apparent to him, as if a veil had been lifted from his eyes.

Jason found Matt within thirty seconds, standing with his pretty girlfriend, Allison Jordan. Although Matt had dated many of the cheerleaders, Ally was surely his trophy.

"Hi, Jay," Ally greeted him with a bright smile. "Are you looking for this guy?" she asked and patted Matt's arm.

Matt turned around and widened his eyes, clearly surprised to see Jason. "What's up? You lost?" he asked as he peered at Jason.

"I need you to help me," Jason replied, keeping his normally loud voice down to a whisper. "I walked into a war zone when I got here this morning. If you haven't heard, there are rumors going around about the fight I got in Friday night. People are saying that I fought O'Leary because he was hitting on my 'secret girlfriend.' I'm pretty confused because I didn't realize I even had a girlfriend, let alone a secret one."

"So, what's your point?" Matt asked impatiently. "Why the hell do you care about what people think?"

"I'm not worried about that. I don't care about what people think of *me*," Jason replied. "Cathy and her friends made up the rumor to torment the girl I defended at the game. I feel horrible because that girl has never spoken a single word to me. Now, everyone is harassing her. They think that I cheated on Cathy with her. I can't stand what they're doing to her."

"They're jealous of her," Ally concluded. "That's what it boils down to."

"I'm kind of surprised you care about this," Matt stated and cocked his head to the side. He looked at Jason thoughtfully. "Who's the girl?"

"Jessie Robins," Jason replied. "She's quiet and keeps herself out of trouble. I threatened Cathy, but there isn't much she can do to stop what's already spreading. She blamed it on her friends."

"Do you want *me* to confront Cathy?" Ally offered willingly.

"No, she's not worth your time," Jason said and shook his head. "Her friends, Lisa Ankerman and Leslie Lucus, are JV cheerleaders."

"Ohhhh," Ally sang and widened her honey-brown eyes. "I see where you're going with this."

Matt rolled his eyes. "You are so lucky to have the connections you have. We'll help you out, but not because I think you need it. I like the fact that you stuck up for that girl, and I'm impressed that you care more about her than your reputation."

Ally nodded in agreement.

"I also don't like it when people try to taint my family's name," Matt added.

"And that is why I love being a Davids!" Jason stated loudly and patted his brother on the shoulder.

Julianna Camen walked into her fourth period Spanish class, trying to forget Jason's warning but failing miserably. *Why would Cathy tell me to sleep next to Marc if he is a womanizer? Why would Marc talk to me all night long if he weren't interested in me? Why does Jason think I'm becoming a mean person? What was the rumor comment about? I only talk to five people on a daily basis; what rumor could I possibly spread?* Julianna was agonizing herself in thought. If Jason was referring to the rumor firing around about him, then he was mistaken. She knew better than to get involved in that mess.

Julianna sat down in her assigned seat and began wondering if Chris was going to say anything to her about Marc. They were close, right? What if Marc had lied about what happened between them? They had only kissed, but Jason had implied otherwise. She would never become a whore! Julianna knew that Cathy and Lisa were not virgins, but they had never put pressure on her to have sex.

"Hi," Chris greeted Julianna with a smile when he walked past her desk.

"Hi," Julianna replied, feeling unworthy of making eye contact with him.

Chris threw a note on Julianna's desk as he passed by. Julianna glanced up in surprise and began unfolding the note.

Julianna,

So hopefully Chris gets this note to you soon. I just wanted to tell you that I had a good time Friday night at the party, and I'm glad you stayed over. My friends thought I was pretty lucky to spend the night with you. You're definitely a cutie. Hopefully we'll hang out again soon. Keep hanging out with Cathy, she knows where to find me. Talk to ya later, Marc

J – I'm sorry I have to give you this. Don't take anything Marc says to heart. He's just a flirt. Praying for you – C

Julianna stared blankly at the paper in front of her. She was happy that Marc had thought of her, but at the same time, she was wary of his motives. If his own cousin was warning her about him, how could she not be? Why did Jason and Chris seem to care more about her wellbeing than Cathy?

A few moments later, Cathy walked into the classroom. For someone whose "boyfriend" had just "cheated" on her, she looked awfully content. Julianna was one of the few people who knew that Jason and Cathy had been on a break for over a week. Cathy had lied to everyone else, claiming that he was still her boyfriend and making him look like a scumbag.

Julianna could not believe that Cathy had the audacity to spread a rumor about Jason. He was not only the boy she claimed to "love," but he was also the scariest person in their grade! *Please don't pull me into the pit you are digging for yourself, Cathy,*

Julianna thought as Cathy walked past her. *I may have picked the wrong—or evil—twin to befriend, after all.*

Chapter 21

Jessie realized it was inevitable; she and Jason would have to talk. Seeing that every time she saw him, she broke out into a sweat and lost her ability to think, she had no idea how a conversation would be possible. Although she had wondered how God would cross their paths, she had never imagined their present dilemma.

Jessie had held her breath when she passed by Cathy in the locker hall. She had expected Cathy to yell at her or at least give her a dirty look. Cathy had done neither. She had peered straight ahead, as if she hadn't even noticed Jessie. Although Jessie was relieved, she wondered why Cathy had spared her. When they had passed by each other, everyone nearby had stopped and stared. Jessie had noticed the disappointed looks on people's faces when Cathy turned the corner without a confrontation.

Katherine Rossi—who typically kept three countries of separation between herself and Jason—asked him to be her partner during their fourth period Geometry class. Jason had been shocked by her proposition and agreed out of sheer curiosity. He assumed that Katherine wanted to talk to him about Jon or, perhaps, his current predicament with Jessie. Either way, he was all ears.

"So, what do I owe this honor?" Jason asked and smirked at Katherine as he opened his book.

"Well, I want a good grade, so I figured I'd ask the smartest kid in class to be my partner," Katherine replied with a shrug.

"Ha, yeah right," Jason said with a short laugh. "I'm a pain to work with; you'll learn that quickly."

Katherine laughed. "OK, so that's not why, but it's still true. I do have an ulterior motive."

Jason laughed, surprised that Katherine was comfortable joking with him. They had hung out a few times in a group setting, but he'd hardly heard her speak more than two words.

"I talked to Jessie this morning, and I told her the same thing," Katherine began, bringing her voice down to a whisper. "I don't agree with what my friends are doing to you guys."

Jason widened his eyes. "I knew it! I knew Lisa and Leslie were behind this!" he exclaimed, feeling extremely proud of himself.

"Shhh," Katherine hushed and slapped Jason lightly on the arm. "I'm only telling you this so you can put a stop to it. Lisa thinks that she is doing the right thing by sticking up for Cathy. She thinks that you really *do* like Jessie and that is why you broke up with Cathy. Then Cathy decided that you had cheated on her. They kept feeding off of each other; it was absurd. Leslie, Julianna, and I are completely skeptical. Even if you did break up with Cathy for Jessie, it doesn't make you a cheater or her a whore."

"No, it doesn't," Jason stated, feeling somewhat redeemed by her words.

"Leslie said that she'd find out if there was anything between you two," Katherine continued, maintaining her whisper. "I guess she has a class with Jessie or something."

"Oh great," Jason said. "I'm sure Jessie's enjoying Leslie's inquiries."

"Julianna and I have *nothing* to do with this," Katherine assured him. "We feel really bad for both of you. Now I know why I never liked Cathy. I know you dated her for a while, and I'm sorry to put her down, but she's pretty evil."

"Oh, without a doubt!" Jason exclaimed and widened his eyes. "Don't waste your time feeling bad for me, though. Feel bad for Leslie and Lisa. They're about to get knocked on their pretty little faces."

Katherine raised her eyebrows and leaned back in her chair. "I told you this because I want you to protect Jessie, not because I want my friends crucified," she said.

"I already knew it was them before you said anything," Jason said and began rolling his pencil up and down his desk. "Besides, how else am I supposed to protect Jessie? Girls like Cathy and Lisa think they're invincible. They're hot, so they think they don't have to be nice. Thank God for girls like you and Jessie, or guys would be flat out of luck. We'd have to choose between 'hot but psycho' or 'nice but ugly.' I'd pass on both and die a bachelor."

Katherine let out a short laugh and then smiled at him. "What happened to you?"

"What's that supposed to mean?" Jason asked with a smirk.

Katherine shrugged. "I don't know, never mind. Maybe I just never really knew what you were about. You seem a lot different from afar."

"Am I going to regret asking how I seem from afar?" Jason questioned her hesitantly.

"Probably," Katherine replied as her cheeks reddened.

"Why am I not surprised?" Jason remarked and rolled his eyes. "You don't have to answer, Katherine Rossi. You're one of the hot-nice girls. I don't want to think of you any other way."

"Thanks," Katherine said and blushed more deeply. "So, what about Cathy? You're just going to let her off the hook?"

"Ha, that would never happen!" Jason stated with amusement. "We've already exchanged some words. Except for the fact that it caused anguish for Jessie, I'm glad Cathy pulled this crap. I can finally see her in clarity. I was too messed up before to realize how ridiculous she was. It's no secret that I'm a jerk when I'm under the influence. She seemed perfectly nice to me."

"So, I take it you won't be getting back together?" Katherine asked and raised her eyebrows at him expectantly.

"This has turned into an awfully deep conversation for math class," Jason said, purposely dodging her question as he began flipping through his book. "Why don't we focus on trapezoid proofs?"

"Sorry," Katherine said. "I just didn't expect you to be so open."

"I'm somewhat shameless," Jason said flatly as he skimmed over his assignment sheet.

"Shameless but not heartless," Katherine stated. "I think most people get that wrong about you."

Jason looked up at Katherine in surprise. "Heartless? People think I'm *heartless*?"

"Well, yeahhh," Katherine sang matter-of-factly.

Jason felt the color drain from his face. "That's crazy! I love people."

Katherine shrugged. "Well, like you said, you can be a jerk when you're messed up. Plus, you tease people constantly. I know you think you're just being funny, but it hurts their feelings."

"Oh, come on," Jason protested. "I've been like this my whole life, and people love me for it. I don't have anything against anyone I tease. People shouldn't take me seriously."

"People are afraid of you for a reason," Katherine said. "I'm sure no one has even given you a hard time about this rumor going around."

Jason shrugged. "People can talk all they want about me. I dish it out, so I can take it. But Jessie, she doesn't deserve it. I get what you're saying, though; I get a little out of control with the rude comments. Nine times out of ten, I'm on something when that stuff comes out of my mouth. I'm not a heartless person, Katherine. In sobriety, I think I'm pretty nice. I just haven't been sober much in the past couple years."

Katherine was staring at him strangely. Jason couldn't understand why she looked so perplexed; everyone in his grade knew he had a drug problem.

"Thanks for telling me all this stuff, though," he said quietly after a moment. "You know, about the girls and even the stuff I didn't want to hear about myself. I kind of need to hear stuff like that. You're actually the second person who's pointed that out to me today."

Katherine's hazel eyes grew wide. "Wow, someone actually stood up to you?" she asked.

"Well, this other person is a *real* piece of work," Jason replied. "She's never had a problem putting me in my place."

"Ohhhh," Katherine sang in recognition. "Our best friend."

Jason nodded. "If I ever became who I wanted to be when I was younger, she would hate me. How can I achieve my goals with her pulling me in the opposite direction? The funny thing is I never even realized she was pulling me that way. I might have been able to ace a test on drugs, but I certainly had a warped perception of myself and my life."

92

Katherine stared at him in silence. "I can relate to you," she said after a moment.

"How is *that* possible?" Jason asked and smiled at her with curiosity.

"We both need to do what my dad calls 'jump out of the boat,'" Katherine replied. "I don't know where he got that expression, but it means to step out of your comfort zone."

Jason raised his eyebrows. "I broke up with mine. Who's in your boat?"

"My problem isn't who's in the boat; it is all the people who aren't," Katherine said.

"What about Jon? Where does he fit into your scenario?" Jason asked.

Katherine blushed and lowered her head. "Jon's nice," she replied quietly.

"He's the man," Jason stated enthusiastically. "Somehow, he puts up with me, Chris, and Bryan. He stayed friends with us without ever lowering himself to our level—kind of like how you are with Lisa and Leslie. You're their friend, but you're different. That's how Jon is in our crew."

"How so?" Katherine asked. "I don't really know much about him."

"Jon's always been against drugs. I think he's smoked weed, like, three times in his life. Chris and I used to smoke three times a day," Jason said. "I haven't seen him drunk once this year. He has a good head on his shoulders. Jon grew up in church and was raised with a lot of morals. When we all went off the deep end last year, trying every drug in sight, he distanced himself from us with Alyssa. It was good they dated."

"You talk like *you* think drugs are bad or something," Katherine said and gazed at Jason skeptically.

Jason let out a deep breath. "I'm not stupid, Kat. I know drugs are bad. I'm just weak to temptation," he admitted. "That's why I had to distance myself from Cathy."

"You surprise me," Katherine said and nodded slowly. "I guess you realize after talking to someone how stupid you were to base your opinion of them on their reputation alone. I bet you never robbed a liquor store either, huh?"

Jason laughed. "Nope," he said. "That rumor even impressed me. Luke and I *did* park Principal Allen's car on the football field, though—obviously Luke drove. But no, I never cheated on Cathy with Alyssa or locked Andy out of the basement during the tornado. None of those rumors are true. No wonder people think I'm heartless. Seriously, my rep is horrible."

"You don't even care, do you?" Katherine asked.

Jason shrugged. "I only care about the opinions of people who know me. My friends know that I'm not heartless, and my parents think I'm the golden child. Besides, the only person who really knows your heart is God. Chris told me that, and it makes sense because people misunderstand each other all the time."

Katherine nodded. "Well, I've already learned more in class today than usual."

Jason smiled, wondering why his perspective on life was changing so drastically.

Chapter 22

At lunch, Jessie took her usual seat beside Sarah at a table full of freshmen girls. As soon as she sat down, all eyes locked on her.

"Does Jason Davids like you?" Jane Sanders asked with wide eyes.

"Are you upset that Cathy Kagelli is mad at you?" Lyndsey Holbrook asked from beside Jane.

"Why did Jason stick up for *you* anyway?" Jaime Campanili questioned her. "He's the most popular boy in our grade. Do you even know him?"

"Don't you care that Lisa Ankerman *hates* you?" Alexis McAndrews asked.

"I don't know Jason," Jessie replied flatly. "I'm not worried about Cathy, Lisa, or anyone's popularity. My friends know the truth, and God knows the truth. So, what do I have to worry about?"

"Yeah, but Jessie, come on!" Alexis sang dramatically. "You must care a little that people are making fun of you!"

"I wouldn't care if people thought I was going out with Jason," Lyndsey piped in.

"He's a drug addict!" Sarah stated loudly.

"Oh please, Sarah," Jaime said and rolled her eyes. "All those boys drink and smoke pot, even the nice ones like Bryan and Andy."

"I doubt Andy Rosetti does drugs!" Sarah exclaimed. "You shouldn't say stuff like that while he's in a coma."

"Sorry," Jaime said sheepishly. "I'm just saying that none of those boys are innocent. Jason's no worse than the rest of his friends. He's just more obnoxious."

"What world are you living in, Jaime?" Laura Johnson spoke up. "Jason's a lot worse than his friends. Chris and Jon are straightedge. The only person worse than Jason is Cathy."

"Guys, stop!" Jessie cried out. "How do you even know all this stuff? Why do you concern yourselves with their business? You talk about them like they're celebrities. Gossip does not edify anyone!"

"And this comes from the girl who everyone's talking about," Alexis commented dryly and rolled her eyes.

"I think it's ridiculous to waste your time talking about them," Jessie stated honestly. "It makes you no better than them. Just because they're in the spotlight doesn't mean you have to pay attention to them constantly! Yeah Lisa, Cathy, Chantal, Alyssa, and Katherine are *really* pretty. Jon, Chris, Jason, Jeff, Andy, and Bryan are *really* cute. Who cares? They're people just like us. I doubt they sit around and talk about you!"

The girls stared at Jessie, seeming to have been silenced by her sudden boldness. Jessie rarely expressed her opinion, let alone so strongly. Her friends' cattiness had finally gotten to her. Even Sarah, who was always opinionated, looked convicted. Jessie knew that her friends were guilty of idolizing the popular people in their grade. In doing so, they had only heightened the divide between cliques.

"I'm going to buy lunch," Jessie stated with annoyance. She stood up from her seat without inviting any of her friends to join her.

"Hey! Jessie!" a loud voice called out from behind her as she neared the lunch line.

Before she could turn around, her cheeks began to burn. As she turned to see Jason entering the cafeteria with Bryan and Jon, she felt a tingly feeling shoot through her body. Jason separated from his friends and began heading toward her. Jessie held her breath as Jason approached her.

"Hey," he said softly with the same look of compassion in his eyes that she had seen at the game.

Jessie stared at him, wide-eyed, trying to find her voice.

"I'd like to eat lunch with you if you would join me?" Jason asked and tilted his head to the side.

Jessie had never expected such a gentle tone of voice to come from Jason's mouth. The warmth that radiated from his blue eyes melted her insides. His eyes were full of sympathy and concern. His gaze was so warm that Jessie swore she saw the love of Christ in him. As far as she knew, that was impossible.

96

Her tongue untied itself, and the tingles throughout her body dissolved. All of her anxiety melted away, and a warm sense of peace rushed through her. The boy that God had given her supernatural concern for, the boy that had been so heavily on her heart for weeks, the boy that she could not be in the same room as without almost fainting—the most beautiful boy she'd ever seen—was standing before her and inviting her to eat lunch with him. Jessie knew that she should have been awestruck and that she should have been weak at the knees or nervously fidgeting, but for some reason, she was calm. "I'd like that," she replied softly and smiled.

A wide grin spread across Jason's attractive face and his blue eyes glistened. "Were you already sitting somewhere?" he asked in the same gentle tone.

"Yeah, I put my stuff down at that table," Jessie said and pointed across the cafeteria.

"Do you still want to sit with your friends? Or can we sit somewhere more private?" Jason asked.

"I think privacy would be better," Jessie replied, imagining her friends' reactions if Jason sat down at their table.

"Do you want me to go get your stuff while you wait in line?" Jason offered. "I brought my lunch today."

Jessie raised her eyebrows, surprised by Jason's considerate offer. "Sure, just ask Sarah for my books," Jessie replied. "You know who she is right?"

"The girl from the game?"

"Yeah, my best friend."

"All right. I'll be back," Jason said and patted her on the shoulder before walking off toward the girls' table. *Wow,* Jessie thought. *That felt so natural.*

As Jason walked across the cafeteria toward Jessie's table, he was aware that most of his grade was watching him. Whenever Jason glanced at people, they dropped their eyes to the floor. *Wow, people really are scared of me,* he thought sadly. *That's awful.*

Katherine's words had impacted him. "Heartless," she had said. Although Jason did not care about what people thought of him, he cared about people thinking that he didn't care about them! He could not understand where "heartless" had come from. He was the most affectionate one of his friends—always hugging people, slapping hands, and patting backs. He had always made it a point to help his friends clean up after their parties. He even took care of them when they got sick. *Heartless?* Jason could not understand it.

He assumed that he looked disturbed when he reached Jessie's lunch table. All seven girls looked up at him with dropped jaws. To Jason's dismay, they seemed horrified by the sight of him. His heart began pounding heavily against his chest, and he suddenly felt like he wanted to cry. *How horrible of a person have I been? So heartless that even these girls are scared of me?* He pasted the friendliest smile he could across his face. "Hi, girls. Uh, I came to get Jessie's stuff," he said slowly and planted his eyes on Sarah.

Sarah raised her eyebrows and remained silent.

"She's going to eat lunch with me today," Jason continued, feeling the need to plead his case. "We have some things to talk about."

"Why would I give you her things?" Sarah questioned him. "Thanks for sticking up for us at the game, but that doesn't mean I have to trust you."

Taken back by Sarah's response, Jason stood in silence.

"Sarah!" Lyndsey Holbrook cried out angrily. "Give Jason her stuff! They *obviously* need to talk."

"Thank you, Lynds!" Jason exclaimed gratefully. He let out a deep breath, happy that someone was showing him favor. He never thought stepping out of his comfort zone would be so convicting. His friends—who were often labeled popular, snobby, and hard to befriend—absolutely adored him. How was it that random people— nobodies on the MLH social scale—could show him such little acceptance? *Shouldn't these people adore me as well?* Jason asked himself. *Am I cocky for thinking that? All I want is Jessie's books! Why am I examining my conscience?*

"Here," Sarah huffed as she slid Jessie's books to the end of the table. "Just don't sell them for drug money."

Jason dropped his jaw and widened his eyes in disbelief. Normally, a comeback—so cruel that it would have sent Sarah off crying—would have rolled off his tongue in a millisecond. Instead,

Jason stared at her blankly, realizing that he hated the person everyone thought he was.

"She's kidding!" one of the girls at the table cried out.

"No worries," Jason said with a laugh. "I stopped by the elementary school this morning and beat up the third graders for their lunch money. I actually beat up the little girls, too, so I'm set for drug money. I hate to hurt little girls, but with the price of coke these days, what else am I supposed to do?"

The girls stared at Jason blankly.

"Thanks for Jessie's books, Sarah," he said calmly and then smiled at her. "And for the record, I usually only beat up the boys. Peace out, ladies!" he laughed and then grabbed Jessie's books off the table before heading toward the lunch line. "Unbelievable," he said beneath his breath, hoping that Jessie's friends had picked up on his sarcasm.

Chapter 23

Jon Anderson sat between Chantal and Bryan at their lunch table, staring over at Katherine. She was sitting beside Bobby at a nearby table, playing distractedly with the food in her dish. Jon did not know how to read Katherine well, but he thought she appeared uncomfortable. Lisa, Leslie, Julianna, and Cathy were sitting on the other side of her, but Katherine had not glanced once in their direction. *She is so much better than her friends. She belongs over here with me,* Jon thought. The other girls were involved in light conversation, which meant Cathy had not noticed Jason sitting with Jessie.

"So, what's going on over there?" Alyssa asked, stealing Jon from his daze as she pointed toward Jason. "Is he really going to eat lunch with her?"

"It looks that way," Jon replied.

"Yeah, he said he wanted to talk to her about *the* rumor," Bryan stated. "I don't think he's over there asking her out or anything."

"That would be funny," Alyssa said with a laugh. "I'd love to hear what they're talking about. He looks kind of into her."

"How can you tell?" Bryan asked.

"You guys are so nosy," Chris said. "Let Jay do his thing. He needs to set things straight for Jessie."

"She was handling it well when I saw her," Marielle said from beside Chris. "She didn't seem to care that everyone was saying horrible things about her."

"I'm sure she cares *a little*," Alyssa said.

"Who wouldn't care if our entire grade was talking about them?" Bryan asked. "Obviously, she cares."

"Jay wouldn't," Jon said flatly, finding the irony of the situation somewhat amusing. "People have been talking about him since he came out of the womb."

"That's true," Bryan agreed. "He is notorious. I'll give him that."

Jon had come to the conclusion that Jason had lost his

mind. *Why is he eating lunch with Jessie? Is he trying to egg on the rumor? What business does he have with her, anyway?* Jon's mind was a barrel of questions as he squinted to get a better view of the interaction between Jason and Jessie. *Jason? With my pastor's daughter? This makes no sense!*

One-month prior, Jason had not only turned on Chris, but also tried to destroy his reputation for getting sober and becoming a Christian. The hostility that Jason harbored toward God and Chris—his best friend since kindergarten—had plagued their group of friends, causing division and turmoil. If it were not for Andy's accident, Jon doubted that Chris and Jason would have ever rekindled their friendship. Believing that he was to blame for Andy's accident, Jason had fled to Chris for help. *Tragedy certainly has a way of bringing people together*, Jon concluded.

"Your sister is going to freak out when she notices Jason sitting with Jessie," Bryan said to Chantal. "I talked to her at the party the other night. She's a mess about their breakup. They were inseparable for two years. Plus, she lost her best friend," Bryan said and nudged Alyssa, "when Alyssa came to her senses and started hanging back out with you."

"Thank God!" Alyssa exclaimed and let out a heavy breath.

"Even though she doesn't show it, I'm sure she feels responsible for what happened to Andy," Marielle reasoned. "I mean she was just as high as Jason. She could have remembered to let your dog in. She could have gone outside to get her. She just sat there, like Jason did, and did nothing. Has she even visited Andy yet?"

Chantal shook her head from side to side. "She won't go with me, Lisa, or Jason," she said sadly. "I believe she has put all of her energy this month into brainwashing Julianna. She has found plenty of satisfaction in stealing her from you guys."

"She's so evil," Bryan said with a laugh. "I can't believe you two came from the same egg. How does that happen?"

Chantal shrugged. "I used to think Jason had corrupted her," she said, "but then I realized that Jason is actually a lot nicer than she is. If anything, she corrupted him."

101

Jon, Chris, and Bryan began laughing and nodding in agreement.

"I think Jay is starting to see through her charm," Chris said. "I've been telling him for a while that she's psychotic."

"Yeah, as long as he is sober," Bryan said. "Once he gets wasted, he wants to go right back to her. I'm so proud of him for leaving her at Samson's Saturday morning. That took a lot of character."

"Maybe all that praying we did helped," Chantal said and glanced from Jon to Chris. After the football game, Jon, Chris, and Chantal had prayed for Jason for over an hour. They had prayed that God would do whatever it took to bring Jason to Christ. They had prayed that the veil Satan had over his eyes would be lifted and that he would begin to see things clearly. They had prayed that he would have the strength to stay away from drugs and that he would realize the emptiness he felt inside was really a hunger for God.

"Cathy, I'm *so* glad you're sitting with us today," Leslie said cheerfully from beside Katherine Rossi. "Seriously, you were in isolation for *way* too long. What the heck, girl! We missed you!"

"Yeah, I know," Cathy said. "I just *had* to pull away from everyone to deal with Jason."

Cathy's melodramatic tone placed a pit in Katherine's stomach. *Why do Lisa and Leslie adore this girl?* she wondered.

"Girl, I have no idea what is going on with Jay, but you're better off without him," Leslie assured her. "He's clearly screwed up. People don't just change overnight like that. I think he had a mental breakdown or something."

Leslie, you have no idea what you are talking about. Just shut up for once! Katherine thought.

"He's been acting weird ever since he started hanging out with Chris again," Cathy stated and flipped her auburn hair over her shoulder. "He actually mentioned God to me."

Lisa, who was sitting beside Cathy, let out a short laugh.

"Are you kidding?" Leslie asked. "Jason? Didn't he start the rumor that Chris joined a cult?"

Cathy laughed. "Yup, same kid."

"I don't get it," Leslie admitted and shook her head. "I heard that Jay feels responsible for what happened to Andy. It's been ever since Andy's accident that he's been acting so weird. That's what got him and Chris to talk again in the first place. I think, if anything, he just wants God to answer our prayers so that Andy will wake up healthy. Maybe he figures God won't forgive him unless he straightens out a bit."

There you go, Lee. You're finally making sense, Katherine thought. *Cathy is going to rip you apart for that one.*

Cathy looked up at Leslie, lowered her eyebrows, and dropped her jaw.

"What?" Leslie questioned her defensively.

"Have you actually thought about this?" Cathy asked accusingly. "Who are you, *Chantal*?"

"Woah, Kagelli back off," Lisa said playfully and nudged Cathy's shoulder. "Way to freak out over nothing!"

"He must have talked to you about this," Leslie pressed, appearing unmoved by Cathy's remark.

Cathy shrugged. "Whatever. I don't understand what is going on with our friends. I miss Chris's parties and Jay's dirty jokes. Jon turned into a complete dork when he broke up with Alyssa. Ugh, and don't even get me started on *her*! Bryan will probably be the next one to change. After all, he is dating that awful Courtney girl. As soon as she entered the picture, our entire social circle decomposed!"

"Yeah, she's not even in this country right now, and things are still whacked out," Lisa agreed.

"We should start hanging out with older guys," Cathy stated enthusiastically. "Like with Luke Davids and Marc Dunkin. I had a good time at Samson's party Friday night. Those kids know how to party. Julie, what did you think?"

"They were cool," Julianna replied quietly, sounding about as enthused by the conversation as Katherine felt.

"You and Marc hit it off," Cathy said in mischievous tone. "Maybe he'll invite us out next weekend!"

"Cathy, those boys are three years older than us, and they're wicked hot!" Lisa cried matter-of-factly. "Do you know how much the senior girls will hate you? You can't just move in on their guys! Ally Jordan, Missy Kent, Michelle Taylor, Katie McKnight, Laurelle Mahoney, Day Angeletti...I could keep going with the names. Those girls are gorgeous and wicked popular; I don't think they'd become your friends. They're basically us, three years from now. If I were Michelle Taylor, wearing the Homecoming crown, I wouldn't give a freshman the time of day!"

"Are you forgetting that I dated Jason for two years?" Cathy asked in a voice full of attitude. "I know his brothers and Ally Jordan pretty well. Luke adores me, and he's dating Missy Kent. I talked to her for a while at the party. She's actually really nice."

"Yeah, but I'm sure Luke had her all coked up," Lisa stated dryly. "She'd never say hi to you in school. Those girls won't even look at me, and I'm a cheerleader. Katherine, do they talk to you during your games?"

"What?" Katherine asked, although she had heard Lisa perfectly clear.

Lisa sighed impatiently. "The senior girls that you cheer with on varsity," she replied. "You know Ally, Missy, Michelle, and all them."

"Oh, they're nice," Katherine replied. "Ally kind of took me under her wing because I'm the only freshman."

"I told you that Ally is awesome!" Cathy exclaimed and slapped Lisa's arm.

"Whatever," Lisa said. "I've never seen them be friendly."

"Well, you're major competition for them," Leslie stated and nodded intently.

"What?" Lisa asked, glaring at Leslie as if she were crazy.

"Sure! You're probably the only girl in this school as pretty as Michelle Taylor," Leslie said.

Lisa laughed. "Stop it! I'm not competition for any of them. Besides, Ally and Missy are just as pretty as Michelle. Maybe in three years I'll compare to them."

"Wow! Humility coming from your mouth? That's priceless," Cathy stated dryly.

Katherine played with her food on her tray, trying to drown out her friends' conversation. Every day it was one of two things:

104

sharing gossip or idolizing the "popular" upperclassmen. When Cathy had come up with the idea of calling themselves the "Fab-5," Katherine had suggested they kept it to four and excluded her. She had told Lisa that she did not want to be linked to anyone by name. Somehow, Lisa had broken the news to Cathy. The truth was that Katherine was nothing like the other four girls and did not want to acquire their reputations.

Normally, Katherine could handle the girls by balancing them out with Bobby. Since Bobby had begun distancing himself from the world, Katherine found herself stuck with only her friends. One-on-one, they were fine, but in a group, she could barely stomach them. Cheerleading had become a great escape for her, and she was relieved that Lisa and Leslie had not made varsity.

Truthfully speaking, Katherine found the varsity cheerleaders to be *a lot* friendlier than her own friends. Katherine had no doubt that Lisa would someday be their homecoming queen and not give a freshman the time of day. Michelle Taylor, on the other hand, had invited Katherine to her upcoming slumber party. Katherine's social anxiety had tempted her to decline, but after pushing past her fear of speaking to Jason, she felt confident enough to accept Michelle's invitation.

She glanced over at Jason's usual lunch table and made eye contact with Jon. She smiled at him, thinking about how much she enjoyed their conversations. She shot her eyes around Jon's table, looking for Jason. Alyssa, Chantal, Marielle, Bryan, Chris, and Jon were engulfed in conversation, but their table was missing three key players: Courtney, Andy, and Jason. It seemed empty compared to Katherine's overstuffed table, and she wished that she had sat with Jon. *Perhaps tomorrow I will dangle my feet in the water*, Katherine thought, *and take one step closer to the edge of my boat.*

Chapter 24

"So, people seem to think we're together or something," Jason said with a laugh. He smiled at Jessie sheepishly. "I can't believe anyone would think you'd give me a chance. You're perfection, and I'm the biggest screw-up around."

Jessie stared at Jason, completely surprised by the boldness of his opening statement. *How could Jason Davids think that I'm perfection? He dated one of the most popular, prettiest girls in our grade for nearly two years. Jason's older brothers dated gorgeous girls, as did all of his friends. How could he compare me to them?* "You don't even know me!" Jessie exclaimed as she stuck her fork through a crouton in her salad. "How can you call me perfection?"

Jason put his sandwich down, cocked his head to the side, and smiled at her. "Jessie, let me tell you something; girls like Cathy and guys like me are a dime a dozen. When I saw you sing at Andy's prayer service, I was awestruck. I saw something in you that I had never seen before. It amazed me," he admitted. "So, I asked Chris about you."

"You noticed me?" Jessie asked, remembering how surprised she had been to see Jason at the prayer service.

"Yeah I *noticed* you," he said, "but I never thought three weeks later we would be in a 'secret relationship!'" Jason laughed and rolled his eyes. "My God, she is so ridiculous."

"Who?" Jessie asked, astounded by Jason's charisma.

"My girlfriend—well *ex-girlfriend,* now," Jason replied. "I'm going to be perfectly honest with you, Jessie, and I don't want you to take offense to anything I say because I have a lot of respect for you. Cathy and her friends started the rumor about us because Cathy is jealous of you. I've been trying to break up with her for the past few weeks, and she hasn't been dealing with it very well. When I wouldn't take her calls, but punched some kid out for you, I think it sent her emotions into the deep end. I'm really sorry that you've been dragged into this. I couldn't care less about people bashing my name, but you don't deserve it. I'm not a jerk like some guys, and I'm not going to sit here and let this happen to you. Yeah, I might be a punk, but I'm not uncompassionate by any means. To you, I must look like a horrible person, I'm sure. Your friend Sarah already insinuated that I wanted your books so I could sell them for drug money. I can only imagine what you think of me if that is her opinion."

Jessie's heart skipped a beat. "She insinuated what?!" she exclaimed.

Jason laughed. "Crazy, right? How dare she not know I'm filthy rich!"

Jessie laughed.

"Joking aside, I can't really blame her. I've probably done more drugs than ninety-nine percent of the kids in this school. That's no secret. It's just funny she said that. I never expected a little girl like her to have so much candor."

"Yeah, that's Sarah," Jessie mumbled. She was surprised that Jason was being so open with her. *More drugs than ninety-nine percent of the school?* Wow, no wonder she felt compelled to pray for him. "My dad used to do drugs when he was our age," she said, hoping that Jason would admit to knowing her father.

"Yeah, I know," Jason replied. "Your dad's a cool guy. He talked to me for a while before Andy's prayer service."

"Is that why you punched that kid? Because you know my dad?" Jessie asked.

Jason blushed slightly and took a sip of his drink. "That's funny you asked," he said and placed his drink on the table. He stared at its label and smiled slightly. "That's what I told Cathy. I told her that your dad helped me out a bit and that I didn't even know you."

"Oh," Jessie said quietly as her stomach dropped.

"What I told Chris is a complete different story," Jason added and glanced up at her. "Both are true."

"I see," Jessie said. For the first time during their conversation, Jessie thought Jason seemed nervous.

"So, uh, I guess I had a few reasons," Jason stated as he peeled the label off of his water bottle.

"Well, what did you tell Chris?" Jessie asked curiously.

"Ha, wouldn't you like to know!" Jason teased her. He smirked at her playfully with twinkling eyes.

Jessie widened her eyes and dropped her jaw in an amused manner. "You really are a jerk, aren't you?" She laughed and tapped Jason lightly on the arm.

"Oh, you have no idea," Jason replied and shook his head. "If I told you any details about myself, you would leave this table."

"I doubt that," Jessie said and crossed her arms.

"I'm not going to risk it. I'm enjoying your company too much," Jason said with a crooked smile.

"You still haven't told me why you punched that kid," Jessie said nonchalantly.

"Oh, that," Jason said and rolled his eyes. "Minor details."

Jessie gazed at Jason in disbelief, accepting that he was never going to tell her his real motive. "So, did you really rob a liquor store?"

"Ha, what?" Jason asked. "No, I've never stolen anything."

"What about the rumor about you and Alyssa?" Jessie asked and raised her eyebrows up and down. "Is that really why Jon broke up with her?"

Jason shook his head from side to side and laughed. "I would never cheat on my girlfriend, especially not with my friend's girlfriend!"

"Hmmm, well that's good," Jessie said. "Do you smoke?"

"Cigarettes?" Jason asked and puckered his lips.

Jessie nodded.

"Nooooo," Jason stressed. "Ugh, that's my pet peeve. People think I smoke? Oh, that's just gross! I've never smoked a cigarette in my life."

"Well, I didn't think you smoked if it makes you feel any better," Jessie stated, happy that she had been right. "People just assume that because of who you hang out with."

"See, I don't really get that," Jason said, sounding somewhat defensive, "because Chris, Jon, and Bryan are my best friends, and they don't smoke. Chris and Bryan used to, but that's history. I bet no one thinks Lisa Ankerman or Leslie Lucus would ever smoke, but I've seen them both do it. Yet, everyone thinks they're *so* clean-cut. I'm not trying to put them down, but my point is that people shouldn't judge a book by its cover. Most of the time reputations are crap."

"I agree with you," Jessie said.

"Sometimes I can be really blunt with my opinions," Jason said. "You'll have to get used to that."

Jessie lowered her eyebrows, wondering what he was insinuating. "Sarah's my best friend, remember? I'm used to strong opinions," she added.

"Oh, that's right, your best friend who loves me," Jason sang and snapped his fingers.

"She's just over-protective," Jessie said. "She's worried about me because of the rumor."

"Yeah, that's what I figured we would talk about. No offense, but I didn't expect you to be so at ease. I thought you would be crying on my shoulder," Jason admitted with a slight shrug.

"It's like what you said; I don't care what people say about me," Jessie stated. "I know the truth, my friends and family know the truth, and God knows the truth. What more could I ask for? Besides, the truth always comes to the light."

"You are probably the strongest girl I've ever met," Jason said with a look of admiration in his eyes.

"I get all my strength from God," Jessie said flatly. "He's good like that."

Jason nodded, while appearing to be in deep thought. "Do you think we could eat lunch together again?" he asked after a moment.

Jessie raised her eyebrows and shrugged. "Sure, anytime."

Jason smiled, again appearing lost in thought. "This was nice," he said after a moment. "I'm glad Luke wanted pizza."

Chapter 25

Ally Jordan and Michelle Taylor left the cafeteria together, deciding to take a detour to their fifth period class. The two girls, both petite in figure with dark brown hair and honey brown eyes, linked arms and entered the Red House of their high school. Realizing how out of place they looked, walking through the freshmen locker hall, the girls couldn't help but laugh. The sea of young faces that moved around them seemed awestruck by their presence.

It was not hard for the girls to locate Lisa and Leslie. They were doing exactly what Jason had predicted: standing in the middle of the hallway with Cathy Kagelli and the girl she had brought to Samson's party. Ally looked at Michelle and rolled her eyes, recalling the girls in their own grade who had once proclaimed themselves as the "Fab-4." Luckily for their class, Ally, Michelle, and their friend Katie McKnight had something against cliques and quickly smothered the Fab-4's fire. Three years later, Ally and Michelle were part of MLH's first class without high walls of social division. As far as they were concerned, this was their last year to make a difference at MLH.

"Hey girls," Michelle said as she stepped in front of Lisa, Leslie, Cathy, and Julianna.

"Hi!" Leslie exclaimed immediately.

"Ally!" Cathy cried out and reached forward to hug her.

Lisa glanced over in surprise and then stared at them strangely. She looked them up and down and then flipped her hair over her shoulder. "Hi," she said after a moment and placed her arms across her chest.

"So, here's the deal," Ally said, after pulling free from Cathy's tight embrace. "We've decided that we need to pull two alternates up from JV to practice with varsity."

"Yeah, with competition coming up we need to have a substitute flyer and base on the squad in case any of the girls get hurt," Michelle added, glancing from Lisa to Leslie.

"The alternates need to practice with us in order to learn our routine," Ally explained. "Lisa, you are the JV flyer with the highest score from tryouts. We think it's only fair to offer you an alternate position."

Lisa raised her eyebrows and looked at Leslie. Leslie widened her eyes and glanced at Ally. Lisa turned back to Ally and Michelle and lowered her eyebrows. "If I practice with you guys, how can I learn my JV routine?" she asked skeptically.

"I'm sure one of your friends could fill you in on everything you miss," Ally reasoned. "It's really not a big deal."

"Lisa you should totally do it!" Leslie exclaimed. "I will teach you our halftime routines. You'll pick them up quickly. You should definitely become an alternate."

Ally glanced at Michelle, surprised by Leslie's enthusiasm and Lisa's lack thereof.

"I guess I'll do it," Lisa said with a shrug. "Learning two halftime routines and training for competition should help keep my mind off of Andy. That could be a good thing."

"Andy?" Michelle asked. "Are you talking about Robby Rosetti's little brother?"

Lisa nodded. "Yeah, he's my best friend."

Michelle pouted. "I'm so sorry. Andy and his family are in my prayers. This must be very hard on you."

Lisa shrugged and looked away from Michelle.

"I know Jason's pretty beat up about the whole thing," Ally said and glanced at Cathy. "He was there when it happened."

"Yeah, at my house!" Cathy exclaimed.

"Oh, you're one of the Kagelli twins," Michelle sang and widened her eyes. "That's right! You were at Ricky's party Friday night with Luke. You date his little brother, don't you?"

"They broke up, Shell," Ally hushed, purposely loud enough for Cathy to hear.

"It's OK; no one knew that until today!" Leslie assured Michelle.

"Well, girls, we're off to class," Ally said and tugged on Michelle's arm. "See you at practice, Lisa."

Lisa stared blankly at Ally for a few seconds and then turned away without saying a word to her.

"That girl is an icicle," Ally said to Michelle, once they were out of the Red House.

"I think she's hurting," Michelle stated. "I think she's hurting and doesn't know how to deal with it. She might be the girl whose dad passed away in that drunk driving accident last summer."

"Oh, really?" Ally asked, trying to recall the accident. "I don't remember that."

"Yeah, Robby told me that it was Andy's best friend's dad," Michelle said.

"Ouch," Ally said. "And now her best friend is in a coma? Yikes. I'm going to find out from Jason if that's true."

"Good idea," Michelle said.

"If it is, I don't think it's the right time to kick her off cheerleading," Ally reasoned.

"Yeah," Michelle agreed. "Maybe instead we can help her deal with everything? She's clearly going through a lot. Maybe that's why this all happened. God works in mysterious ways, you know."

Ally squinted at Michelle and laughed. "I love you, Shell," she said. "You are probably the most optimistic person on earth."

"So, you had lunch with Jessie," Jon said to Jason as they jogged side by side around the indoor track. "How'd it go?"

"She's cool," Jason replied and picked up his pace. "I think my lungs have better capacity since I stopped smoking weed. I feel like I could run around here all day."

"Dude, you always do that!" Jon cried. "You change the subject every time someone brings up Jessie."

"Ha, so," Jason laughed. "I don't want to talk about her."

"Why not?" Jon asked impatiently. "I can't figure you out lately. You're like three different people at once."

"What is *that* supposed to mean?" Jason questioned him.

"You can't just go from dating *Cathy Kagelli* to eating lunch with *Jessie Robins*!" Jon exclaimed matter-of-factly.

"Why not?"

"Dude! Jessie doesn't even swear. She's as innocent as they come. What could you possibly want from her?" Jon questioned him.

"I don't want anything from her," Jason replied flatly. "Why do you think I want something from her?"

"I don't know, because I know you!" Jon cried out.

Jason rolled his eyes and shook his head. "I'm not looking for sex," he said after a moment. "I'm not even looking for a girlfriend right now. All I'm trying to do is figure myself out. I'm seeing things from a different perspective lately, and I have no idea why. I'm just going through something that I really don't want to talk about during gym. Trust me, I'm not trying to take advantage of Jessie in any way. I wouldn't do that."

Chapter 26

Lisa, Cathy, and Julianna stumbled into their sixth period computer class, laughing loudly at their own clumsiness. Jason, who was already seated with Leslie, Jon, and Bobby, nodded toward the girls and rolled his eyes.

"They're baked," Leslie said and shook her head disapprovingly.

"Ladies, please take your seats. Class is about to start," their teacher, Miss Donovan, said calmly.

Jason watched as Cathy, Lisa, and Julianna slowly took their seats. They refused to make eye contact with Miss Donovan. "You look Chinese!" Lisa exclaimed. Jason assumed that she was speaking to Julianna, whose eyes could have been blindfolded with dental floss.

"Miss Ankerman, do you have something to share with the class?" Miss Donovan questioned her suspiciously. "Or would it be OK for me to begin attendance?"

"Yeah, you should probably do that," Lisa said and placed her head in her hands.

Miss Donovan rolled her eyes and began calling out names.

"I've never seen Lisa so giddy," Jon said quietly to Jason after their names had been called.

"They probably smoked an entire quarter or something laced," Jason reasoned. He glanced over at Cathy. She was staring into her compact mirror. By the time Miss Donovan completed attendance, Cathy had applied a fresh coat of lip-gloss, mascara, and eye shadow. Jason raised his eyebrows and turned to Jon. "She's even vain while baked out of her mind," he whispered and nodded toward Cathy.

Jason glanced from Cathy to Chantal, who was sitting across the room with Marielle. Chantal was sitting with her arms crossed, shaking her head in disgust. After a moment, she looked up at Jason and shrugged. Marielle was staring in disbelief at Julianna—her childhood best friend. It had not taken long for Cathy to turn Julianna into one of her protégés.

"Class, go to your assigned computers and open up Adobe InDesign," Miss Donovan instructed. "We're going to work on layouts today."

Jason rested his head in his hands and let out a loud sigh. At the beginning of the term, he had chosen a computer next to Cathy. Spending forty minutes next to her was going to feel like a decade.

"Actually, Lisa and Cathaleen, I would like to separate you two," Miss Donovan said suddenly. "Cathaleen why don't you switch places with Sarah? And Lisa, switch with Bobby."

"Are you serious? I have to sit with those dorks?" Cathy called out loudly as she pulled her long shiny hair into a ponytail. "So lame."

"Ha, you're actually better off," Lisa said. "Now you don't have to sit next to your cheater of an ex-boyfriend."

Jason raised his eyebrows and watched Lisa slip into Bobby's old seat beside Chantal. He began wondering if Ally had spoken with Lisa and Leslie yet. After his conversation with Katherine, he had decided that the heat should be laid most heavily on Lisa. If Leslie had been skeptical of Cathy's lies, then Jason was skeptical of her involvement.

"I want to get the scoop from Jessie about her lunch with Jay," Alyssa said to Katherine as they walked around the gym's indoor track.

"What lunch?" Katherine asked and cocked her head to the side.

"Oh," Alyssa laughed, "you won't believe it, but Jason ate lunch with Jessie today."

Katherine raised her eyebrows and smiled slightly. "That's interesting," she said quietly.

"Yeah, they certainly aren't worried about the rumors circulating. It made us think that he really does like her, and we're his friends!" Alyssa exclaimed. "He makes less sense sober than he did on drugs."

"I thought something seemed different about him," Katherine said slowly. "Did he really stop doing drugs?"

115

"Well, Friday night he juiced himself up on vodka and Vicodin. I guess Matt almost took him to the hospital," Alyssa replied dryly. "But, supposedly, he hasn't gotten high in a week, and he stopped blowing things."

"He was blowing things?" Katherine asked, horrified by the thought. "Like what? Like coke?"

"No," Alyssa replied and shook her head quickly. "He's kept himself away from that, surprisingly, but he developed a fetish for snorting Adderall and probably some other stuff. Whatever he got Cathy into turned her into a horrible person."

"She wasn't always like that?" Katherine asked.

Alyssa scoffed. "No! Not at all. When we became best friends, she was just as sweet as Chantal."

"I can't even picture that."

"Cathy was awesome. She and Jay were, like, the perfect couple before they got into drugs."

"When did Cathy start doing drugs?" Katherine asked curiously.

"Jay and Chris got her and Lisa into weed last year. Jay was trying to help Cathy treat an anxiety problem; Chris was trying to help Lisa grieve her father's death. The boys meant well, but they made dumb choices. Chris has a lot of regrets, and I think Jay does, too."

"Well, Jeff's good for Lisa," Katherine remarked. "He hates drugs, so he's been trying to get her to stop smoking weed."

"Good luck to him; Lisa's wicked stubborn. It wasn't weed that ruined Cathy. She was still a nice person up until a couple of months ago. I think that's when Jay got her into pills."

"I knew Jay smoked a lot of pot, but I never knew he messed with pills until Jeff's bonfire mishap," Katherine said.

"That's when Cathy started acting weird—right after Jeff accidently took Vicodin," Alyssa recalled. "Cathy got wicked stressed out about Jason using painkillers. I begged her to break up with him—Lisa did, too—but she loved him too much to let go. I think she started taking something stronger than weed for her anxiety, and I think that's what changed her personality. She is a *nasty* person right now. I really don't know why Lisa, Leslie, and Julianna are still friends with her."

"My guess is they know what's going on in her life, and they're trying to help her," Katherine reasoned.

"Maybe," Alyssa said with a shrug.

"So, you think Cathy's still into pills, but Jay's clean?" Katherine asked.

"Jay stopped snorting the stuff, but I'm sure he still takes it," Alyssa replied. "He's prescribed Adderall, and obviously he's still popping Vicodin. Jon, Chantal, and Chris are really worried about him, but it seems like he wants to straighten out. It's weird, though. Chris was open with everyone about going straightedge, but Jay is keeping stuff from us. He won't tell anyone what his connection is to Jessie."

"I think that's sweet," Katherine said. "Maybe he really likes her."

"Are you kidding?" Alyssa asked and then laughed loudly. "She's a choir girl! I mean, she's nice, but Jay is *Jay*! He's got to live up to his brothers' standards."

"That's so mean!" Katherine protested. "I think Jessie surpasses Luke and Matt's standards. I know their girlfriends, and even though I like Ally a lot, I think Jessie has more to offer."

"What, like, her virginity and Bible verses?" Alyssa questioned her sarcastically. "You really think *Jason* cares about that stuff?"

"You know him better than I do, but yes, I think he does," Katherine replied and picked up her pace.

"She wouldn't be allowed to date him anyway," Alyssa said once she caught up to Katherine. "There's no way her father would ever approve of Jason."

"That's too bad," Katherine said. "Jason has more potential than any other guy in our grade. He's an absolute genius. If he ever got his head on straight, he could make a big difference in this school. Just look at the impact Chris has had on people. Jason has an even bigger influence than Chris because Luke and Matt are so popular. People's eyes are always on the Davids boys. I cannot fathom the amount of good that could come from Jason cleaning up his act."

"Kat, I think we're talking about two completely different Jason's," Alyssa said. "Your Jason sounds like Chantal's Jason; she's all about him becoming something great. She said God has been ministering to her about him. I don't always understand her, but I know she has good intentions."

"I wish I knew Chantal better," Katherine admitted. "Bobby is Andy's best friend, so you would think we'd be close. I think she shies away from me because I am best friends with Lisa and Leslie."

"She might," Alyssa said, "because you're always with them, and they're always with Cathy. Cathy treats Chantal terribly. She hates her. In seventh grade, she pretended to be Chantal and broke up with Jon. Then she convinced her that Jon cheated on her with me."

"What?!" Katherine cried, wondering how badly Alyssa was exaggerating. Although Katherine liked Alyssa, she knew Alyssa was a busybody.

"Yup! Chantal believed Cathy and had no interest in hearing out Jon or me," Alyssa continued. "Jon and I didn't know that Cathy had lied to Chantal or that Cathy had pretended to be Chantal. We thought Chantal broke up with Jon because he smoked weed at a party. Jon was heartbroken. I was his best friend, so he turned to me for support. We eventually ended up dating, which only made Cathy's story sound more believable. The truth came out last month, after Andy slipped into a coma. It's crazy. Chantal has been through so much."

"Wow. I guess so! So, Jon thought Chantal broke up with him because he started partying? I thought Jon was straightedge?" Katherine asked.

"He was always against drugs, but then curiosity got the best of him. So, he tried a couple of things, which made Chantal really upset. After losing her, he realized that drugs brought nothing but destruction to his life, and he went completely straightedge," Alyssa explained. "Even though he partied with everyone last year, he never took a sip of alcohol. Jon's different from his friends."

Katherine liked everything she had heard about Jon's character. "Why did you guys break up?" she asked curiously.

"That was one of the worst nights of my life," Alyssa stated flatly. "It was my fault. I started doing stuff that I shouldn't have been doing, and Jon felt like he didn't know me anymore. It was an embarrassing wakeup call."

"But you guys are friends now?" Katherine questioned her.

"Yeah, we made up after Andy's accident, after I became friends with Chantal again," Alyssa replied.

"I'm impressed by how well Chantal has handled everything with Andy," Katherine said. "It's inspiring. I can't believe how strong she is. Bobby told me that Chantal has no doubt Andy will wake up. She told him that God will wake Andy up once His work is complete. It's like she sees Andy's coma in a completely different light than the rest of us."

"Yeah, she does," Alyssa agreed. "She prays to God about everything. She believes everything happens for a reason that we don't need to understand. It's hard for me to understand why she thinks what she thinks, but I can't deny the strength she exhibits in all situations. She's content while her boyfriend is on his deathbed. That's just unnatural. She's focused on the way God is using the situation to work in people's lives. She told me the same thing that she told Bobby. She said Andy will wake up in God's perfect timing."

"That's amazing," Katherine said and shook her head in awe. "Doesn't that make *you* want a relationship with God?"

"Well," Alyssa said, "it's gotten me to go to church."

"Hmmm," Katherine murmured, "perhaps God *is* at work here."

Alyssa laughed. "I can tell you've been talking to Jon!"

Katherine felt her face flush. "Yeah, he likes to talk about his faith."

"Why don't you hang out with us outside of school? Like with Jon, Chantal, Chris, Marielle, and me? I think you fit in better with us than with Lisa and Cathy," Alyssa pointed out.

"I'd be up for that," Katherine replied and smiled appreciatively at Alyssa.

Chapter 27

Jason staggered into his eighth period drafting class, wondering how a single day could feel so long. Taking a seat beside Jeff, Jason put his head down on his drafting table. He couldn't wait to go home and sleep.

"Jay, what's the deal?" Jeff asked and slapped Jason lightly across the head.

"What was that for?" Jason asked as he lifted his head off the table and leaned back in his chair.

"You're slipping, man," Jeff stated and shook his head disapprovingly. "You ate lunch with that church-girl? What were you thinking? People with your rep don't lower themselves to that level."

Jason raised his eyebrows and gazed at Jeff in disbelief. Since when did Jeff have the bravado to chastise him? Why had Jeff's words bothered Jason? Jason did not care about his reputation, right? He could eat lunch with whomever he wished, couldn't he? People would still respect him, wouldn't they? He was *Jason Davids*—Matt and Luke's younger brother—how could they not?

"Why are you looking at me like that?" Jeff questioned him. "You'd be the first to ream out any of us for doing that. You talked all that crap about Chris, and now you're chilling with his pastor's daughter? What is going on with you? You can't do that."

"I had to make sure Jessie knew it was just a rumor," Jason said and turned away from Jeff.

"That's crap! If it weren't true, she would have already known," Jeff replied.

Jason laughed. "Yeah, but what if she thought I liked her? I only punched Sean because her dad helped us out with Andy's prayer service. I respect the guy."

"That *was* cool of him," Jeff agreed and lightened his tone. "So, you're not pulling a one-eighty like Chris? We're all getting concerned."

"No!" Jason exclaimed and rolled his eyes. "No way, dude."

"Then are you up for eating 'shrooms right now?" Jeff asked.

Jason widened his eyes and swallowed deeply. "What, dude? You have 'shrooms?"

"Yeah. Let's just do it," Jeff said. "I've got nothing to do after school. Do you?"

Jason racked his brain for any trace of an excuse. How had he pinned himself into a corner? Was Jeff testing him? Since when did Jeff trip? Jeff was class treasurer and a varsity soccer player—someone who could not afford to get caught on drugs. He was best friends with Adam Case, Bobby Ryan, and Andy Rosetti—good kids. He had only become friends with Jason through Lisa. In Jason's eyes, Jeff was a goody-goody. Jason, Chris, Bryan, and Jon had been known as the rebels in their grade for so long that seeing people replace them was beginning to bother Jason. Cathy and Lisa's friendship had caused a merger of cliques, something Jason had previously viewed as a good thing. Now, he begged to differ.

Jeff laughed and clapped his hands together. "Your expression is so priceless right now!" he exclaimed. "I'm kidding, guy. I can't trip in school! That's your forte, not mine."

Jason let out a sigh of relief. "I haven't even done that recently."

"But seriously, what are you doing after school?" Jeff asked. "I'm game for eating them. I bet Sartelli would be up for it, too."

A large lump formed in Jason's throat. Why was he finding it so hard to say no? He had been able to say no to Luke, so why was Jeff a stumbling block? Jeff was his boy—someone he should be able to be honest with. He already felt horrible for lying about his feelings for Jessie. He felt even worse about not sticking up for her.

Jason suddenly felt like a piece of rope in a tug-o-war. Matt's words began ringing through his head, *"Ten years down the road, none of the parties, the drugs, or your high school reputation are going to mean anything to you. If you felt pressured to live up to me and Luke, your thought process is all messed up. You have surpassed both of us already, on so many different levels."*

Jason studied Jeff's facial expression and body language for a couple of seconds. "I don't know if I'm up for eating shrooms," he said after swallowing a large lump in his throat, "but I know you're definitely not."

121

Jeff laughed and turned away from Jason.

"You would never eat mushrooms. You don't even smoke weed. Lisa put you up to this because Cathy wants to know if I'm serious about getting sober. Am I right?"

Jeff smiled. "You know my girlfriend too well," he remarked.

"Your girlfriend was blazed out of her mind today in computer class," Jason said. "It was so obvious. I can't believe Miss Donovan didn't kick her out of class."

"Really?" Jeff asked, looking disturbed by the news.

Jason nodded.

"She's got to watch that," Jeff stated and shook his head. "She could get kicked off student council and cheerleading. She's a mess about Andy and not thinking straight."

"Yeah. Ally doesn't tolerate much crap when it comes to the cheerleaders," Jason said. "She and Matt are both against drugs."

"How does that happen?" Jeff asked. "How did Matt end up with brothers like you and Luke?"

Jason glanced at Jeff blankly, once again hating the person everyone thought he was. Even his friends thought he was more like Luke than Matt. Why wouldn't they? Matt would have said no, without a second thought, to Jeff's after-school offer.

"Excuse me, class," the assistant principal called loudly as he entered the classroom. "Mr. Andrews is out sick today, so you will need to report to study hall in Room 206. You may stop at your lockers for your books."

Jeff nudged Jason. "We can *so* get away with skipping."

Jason stood up reluctantly from his chair. "Nah, dude. I'd rather sleep in study hall," he said, throwing his backpack over his shoulder. "I have a lot on my mind."

"Oooh, like your secret girlfriend, Jay-dawg?" Jeff teased Jason and patted him on the back.

"Yeah, exactly," Jason replied as he followed the rest of his class out of the room. Jason and Jeff separated from their class and headed toward the freshmen locker hall. As Jason opened his locker, a note fell at his feet. Bending over to pick it up, Jason felt his heart begin to race. *Another note?* He still had the other two saved in his bookbag. *Who could possibly be taking such an interest in my life?*

Jeff appeared at Jason's side. "What's that? A love note from Jessie?" he laughed.

Quickly, Jason threw the note in his pocket and grabbed his English book from his locker. "I skipped first period this morning and had breakfast with Luke, Marc Dunkin, Missy Kent, Laurelle Mahoney, and Pat Ryan. It's good we have study hall; I need to catch up on the work I missed," Jason stated as he shut his locker, purposely ignoring Jeff's question.

"It must be sweet to hang out with upperclassmen," Jeff said.

"Eh, whatever. Those kids have been over my house a million times," Jason said carelessly. "Luke kidnapped me. I honestly wanted no part in it."

"You're crazy, dude," Jeff said. "Their girls are so hot. I can't wait to see what Lisa, Alyssa, Courtney, Katherine, and the Kagellis will look like when we're seniors. They're going to be so hot."

"I think Chris did a good job with Marielle," Jason remarked as he entered the stairwell to the second floor. "She's cute, too."

"Yeah, that's right," Jeff agreed. "I know you hate her, but Julianna isn't bad either."

Jason rolled his eyes. "I don't hate her; I hate what Cathy is doing to her."

"Oh, right, I forgot. You suddenly have a soft spot for goody-goodies," Jeff teased him.

"Shut up," Jason retorted. "*You're* a goody-goody, and you know where I stand with Cathy. The last thing this school needs is someone else trying to act like her."

Jeff laughed. "We call Julianna 'Alyssa the Second.'"

"Yup," Jason said carelessly, while taking a seat toward the back of the study hall. All he wanted to do was read the note in his pocket. He had purposely sat where the next available seat was far away. The last thing he wanted was more of Jeff's questions firing at him.

Once everyone around him seemed preoccupied with work, Jason pulled the note out of his pocket. Quietly, he unfolded it, immediately recognizing the handwriting from the first two notes. He smiled and began reading:

"Welcome to the planet... Welcome to existence... Everyone's here... Everyone's here... Everybody's watching you now... Everybody waits for you now... What happens next? What happens next? I dare you to move... I dare you to move... I dare you to lift yourself up off the floor... I dare you to move... I dare you to move... Like today never happened... Today never happened before...

Welcome to the fallout! Welcome to resistance... The tension is here... The tension is here... <u>Between who you are and who you could be</u>... Between how it <u>is</u> and how it <u>should be</u>... I dare you to move... I dare you to move... I dare you to lift yourself up off the floor... I dare you to move... I dare you to move... Like today never happened... Today never happened before...

Maybe <u>redemption</u> has stories to tell... Maybe <u>forgiveness</u> is right where you fell... Where can you run to <u>escape from yourself</u>? Where you gonna go? Where you gonna go? <u>Salvation is here</u>...

I dare you to move... I dare you to move... <u>I dare you to lift yourself up off the floor</u>... I dare you to move... I dare you to move... Like today never happened... Today never happened... Today never happened... Today never happened before."

---

* *Lyrics from Switchfoot's "Dare You to Move"*

Chapter 28

Jessie walked into her eighth period health class right behind Cathy and Julianna—awkward! She spotted Marielle and Chantal sitting with Chris Dunkin and Bobby Ryan in the back-left corner of the classroom. Jessie pondered over sitting in her usual seat in the front-left corner or moving toward the back. She did not want to impose on Chantal and Marielle.

Jessie took her usual seat and placed her books on the floor. Cathy and Julianna were sitting on the right-hand side of the classroom, blatantly glaring at her.

"Hey, Jessie!" a friendly voice cried out.

Jessie turned around slowly and saw Chris waving at her. "Hi," Jessie replied and waved back.

"Come sit with us," Chantal said.

"Oh, of course *Chantal* wants to become friends with her," Cathy said loudly. "Thanks, sis."

"I'm already friends with her!" Chantal retorted.

Jessie, who had begun gathering her books, paused at the sound of Chantal's words. Chantal had been Jessie's friend up until seventh grade when she began dating Jon Anderson. After that, Jon and his friends had consumed all of Chantal's time. However, Jessie was beginning to realize that Chantal had not deliberately abandoned their friendship.

"Oh, that's right!" Cathy sang. "You're sisters in Christ. That's cute."

"Yes, we are," Chantal responded sternly, while maintaining her calm disposition. "Once upon a time, you and Jessie were close, too. She was your friend before you had Jason, before you were popular, and before you changed into someone I can't even recognize."

"Chantal, don't even bother with her," Marielle said and placed her hand on Chantal's shoulder. "She's just jealous and bitter."

Chantal walked past Marielle to Cathy's desk and placed her arms across her chest. "You know bitterness is like drinking poison

125

and waiting for the other person to die," she stated and gazed at her caustic identical twin. "You're destroying yourself from the inside out with bitterness, pride, jealousy, and resentment."

Cathy laughed and turned away from Chantal.

"I hate seeing you put yourself through this! When is it going to stop? What happened to you? Why are you so full of hatred toward everyone who doesn't parade after you? Can't you see that you're pushing everyone who cares about you away?" Chantal continued, slightly raising her voice. "Do you know how much Jason loves you? Do you even realize what you have done to him? What is it going to take to wake you up? Are you dead, Cath?"

Cathy looked mortified when she turned back toward Chantal.

"You're crazy," Cathy said in a calm but patronizing tone. "It's really sad to see you so deranged. You should stick to the other brainwashed people in this room. They're just as crazy as you are, so they think you're kind of normal," she said and smiled sweetly.

Chantal abruptly turned away from Cathy and walked back to her seat. Marielle, Jessie, Chris, and Bobby stared at her with concern. Chantal smiled back at them, as if the conversation had gone well.

"Are you all right?" Marielle asked.

"Oh, yeah," Chantal replied and nodded intently.

"Well, you're probably the first person to stand up to her in a long time," Bobby commented and nodded toward Cathy.

"Actually, Jay took a swing at her this morning," Chris said loudly. "Not literally, of course, but they exchanged some words."

Jessie glanced at Cathy, finally understanding why she had spared her in the hallway earlier. Jason was proving himself to be much more of a stand-up guy than she had ever expected. Actually, Jason had been nothing like she expected. Jessie's mind began spinning as she lost herself in thoughts of him. *Stop, Jessie. It's dangerous to let your mind run away with possibilities. Things are rarely what they seem.* At a young age, she had learned to wait for God's revealing of the truth instead of tormenting herself with analytical misconceptions.

chapter 29

After school, in the girl's locker room, Lisa Ankerman changed out of her black dress pants and fitted turquoise sweater. All fronts aside, Lisa was nervous; practicing with the varsity cheerleaders meant that she would be surrounded by a bunch of girls who thought nothing of her. They were older, prettier, more popular, and more talented than Lisa thought she was. Although practicing with varsity made her look superior to everyone on her own squad, to the varsity cheerleaders, she would seem like nothing more than a wannabe.

After putting on a pair of warm-up pants, Lisa glanced at the t-shirt she had planned on wearing. Leslie had given it to her for her birthday, and Lisa had always been proud to wear it. On the shirt was a picture of Lisa, Leslie, Cathy, Alyssa, Jason, Chris, Jon, Bryan, and Jeff from an eighth-grade party. The caption below read: "If You Don't Love Us Already, You Will!" Flaunting her friends' popularity around the JV cheerleaders had given Lisa a defense mechanism. She wanted people to be intimidated by her. She wanted people to think she was a snob. She did not want anyone trying to befriend her. Lisa had realized after her father's death that the less people she allowed into her heart, the less chance she had of getting hurt. Her true emotions petrified her, and she fought every day to keep them bottled up. Andy was the only person she had ever confided in; without him around, Lisa found herself desperately seeking escapes from reality.

Lisa swallowed the large lump in her throat and pulled the t-shirt over her head. The friends on her shirt, her acclaimed beauty, and her snobby attitude would not intimidate any of the varsity cheerleaders. How could she be rude to them without impeding her chances of making varsity next season?

Being friendly meant letting her guard down—something she did not want to do. Lisa had never understood Leslie and Andy's social abilities. Although she realized that they both were masters of false fronts, she was amazed by the way they could charm a crowd. Being outgoing and unbiased, they made everyone believe that they were exceptionally good people. Their reputations disguised all of their flaws. Lisa, on the contrary, disguised the goodness of her heart by pretending to be callous. She rolled her eyes, imagining how much better high school would be if everyone was real—real like Chris Dunkin. Since his transformation, they had grown apart, but the amount of respect Lisa held for him had tripled.

Glancing one last time at her reflection in the mirror, Lisa stepped out of the small changing room and headed toward the gym. She spotted Katherine stretching by the bleachers and began heading her way. Katherine looked startled by Lisa's presence.

"Lis, what are you doing in here?" Katherine asked. "Is JV practicing with us today?"

"No," Lisa replied and took a seat beside Katherine, "but I was invited to. Ally Jordan and Michelle Taylor came up to me today and said you guys need an alternate for competition."

"Really?" Katherine asked, looking skeptical. "So, did you volunteer, or did they pick you?"

"They picked me," Lisa replied and smiled brightly. "They said that I was the flyer with the highest score from tryouts."

Katherine lowered her eyebrows. "Didn't Chantal have a higher score than you?"

"Yeah, but she's not a flyer," Lisa responded matter-of-factly. "She's not a base either; she's a spotter."

"It's too bad we don't need a spotter," Katherine muttered as she leaned forward in her stretch.

"I guess they asked one of the sophomore bases," Lisa said and glided her legs into a split.

"Well, you'll get to meet the girls you were talking about at lunch," Katherine stated, sounding more annoyed than usual. "Are you nervous?"

"No!" Lisa replied immediately. "They invited *me* here. Why would I be nervous?"

Katherine shrugged. "I don't know. I was nervous at first."

"Well, you get anxiety over this kind of stuff," Lisa said and touched her hands to her toes.

"I'm getting better with that," Katherine said flatly.

Fifteen minutes later, Lisa and Katherine gathered with the rest of the varsity cheerleaders. Lisa glanced at the unfamiliar faces around her, grateful to have Katherine by her side—even though she seemed moodier than usual.

Lisa stared for a moment at Michelle Taylor, wondering how her friends could think she was nearly as beautiful. Michelle had somewhat of an exotic look to her, with long dark brown hair. Michelle was petit in figure with a warm smile and twinkling eyes. She seemed to wear her heart on her sleeve, fearlessly—something Lisa could not comprehend.

"OK, girls. Before we start arm drills, I want to point out Natalie and Lisa to you," Ally called out loudly. "They are from JV, and they're going to train with us for competition. It is just a precaution in case anyone gets hurt. We don't want to be stuck like last year."

"Yeah, you don't need to bring that up," Michelle said and let out a heavy breath.

"They dropped her while practicing fifteen minutes before they were supposed to compete," Katherine whispered to Lisa. "She sprained her wrist and broke her ankle."

Lisa widened her eyes.

"Lisa is a freshman, and Natalie is a sophomore," Ally continued. "They won't be cheering with us at games, but you should make it a point to get to know them. They might be holding you up or starring in your stunt someday. We are a team, and there is no room for animosity."

"Where are Missy and Laurelle?" Katie McKnight, another beautiful senior, asked.

"They're not coming today, but we'll talk about that later," Michelle replied abruptly.

"Well, that's perfect for today then. Lisa can take Missy's spot, and Natalie can take Laurelle's," Ally stated, appearing unconcerned by her friends' noticeable absences. "Line up in rows of two, and let's get started."

"Denise, don't make our arms fall off today!" Katie whined to their coach.

After fifteen minutes of arm drills, Lisa decided that Denise had ignored Katie's mercy plea. Her arms had begun burning after the first five minutes, and they had slipped out of place twice.

"This is why I encourage weightlifting," Ally called out, dropping her arms to her sides. "Clearly, I don't listen to myself enough." Once Ally dropped her arms, the rest of the girls followed. Loud sighs of relief were heard throughout the gym.

"If you want to place in competition, then you need to spend more time lifting," Denise exhorted them, eyeing the girls sternly. "I'm going to add another two minutes to arm drills every week until competition. If your arms slip, then I will know you are not doing your part outside of practice. The weight room is open until eight o'clock every night; take advantage of that. Now that we are in competition training, Wednesday practices will be an extra hour long. Also, Ally and I have decided that we need to enforce our drug policy more strongly. I understand that you girls like to party after the games but be wise; don't drink the night before a game or the day of a game. Anyone caught smoking or vaping will be suspended from the squad. If we have any reason to believe that one of you may have done an illegal substance, we will give you two choices: you can take a voluntary drug test and prove us wrong or you can resign from the squad. There have been too many rumors flying around this school about drug use, and this squad has zero tolerance."

"That's right, girls," Ally agreed and nodded intently. "Ask yourselves what is more important, and don't waste your time practicing for something your heart is not fully in. Competition training is intense. You need to be dedicated to doing what is best for the squad. Don't think for a second that any of you are too valuable to replace. I'm your captain, and I know Michelle or Katie could replace me in a second."

"We wouldn't want to!" Katie cried out.

"You get my point," Ally said. "OK, our arms should be rested by now. Michelle, Katie, and I are going to show you the dance that we've come up with. Hopefully, you can all have it down-pat by the end of this week."

Denise turned on a nearby iPod dock, and loud EDM burst out of the speaker.

"Five, six, seven, eight," Michelle counted to the beat of the music.

Suddenly, Michelle, Ally, and Katie lunged into the fastest routine Lisa had ever seen. It looked amazing! But was it logical for Lisa to spend time learning such a difficult routine that she may never perform? She was somewhat stunned by Ally's impressive rhythm and even more stunned by her anti-drug attitude. Wasn't she good friends with Missy and Luke? Hadn't Jason said they were at a rave today? How could someone on *this* squad skip practice to roll on ecstasy? Was that why Denise gave such a stern talk? Did she know? Lisa's mind raced with questions, wondering if she would have to turn straightedge.

Lisa was against alcohol and most drugs, but weed had become her comfort zone and escape from reality. Lisa realized that if she got caught high, then Denise's view of her would be permanently tainted, which could ruin her chances of ever becoming a captain. If she resigned from being an alternate, then it would be obvious that she had a drug problem. Suddenly, Lisa found herself stuck between a rock and a hard place.

Chapter 30

When Jason arrived home from school on Tuesday, he quickly made way to his large bedroom. His parents were still at work, Matt was at football practice, and Luke was in Springfield. Having the house to himself gave Jason the perfect opportunity to unnoticeably get high. Whether he came home and smoked a bowl or took pills, Jason had been winding down from school with the aid of drugs for the past few months. Today had felt like an extremely long day, and being tempted with ecstasy and mushrooms had not made his day any easier.

Because no one was home, Jason could easily reach into his desk drawer and pull out a bag of weed. Within two minutes, he could be getting high and smoking all of his cares away. Jason sat on his bed and rested his head in his hands. He wanted to overcome his drug habits more than anything, but he had begun to think that he lacked the necessary willpower. *Chris made it look so easy.*

Jason thought of swallowing his pride and calling Chris for help. It seemed like a good idea until he remembered that Chris had football practice until five. Jason sighed and lay down on his bed. He stared up blankly at the ceiling. *Your entire school thinks you're a heartless, drug addict, cheater of a boyfriend*, he thought to himself. *You should just slip back into the daze you've been in for the past two years. None of that ever bothered you when you were high all the time.*

Jason rolled over on his side and glanced at his desk. He pondered for a moment, trying to think of a way to flee from temptation. *I could go for a run*, he thought, *or invite Jon over.* Jason reached for his phone and dialed Jon's number. Immediately, he reached Jon's voicemail. After ending the call without leaving a message, Jason dialed Jon's landline. After the Anderson's answering machine picked up, Jason grew discouraged. He placed the phone down on his bed and brought his hands to his forehead. "I'm driving myself crazy," he moaned.

A moment later Jason rose from his bed and took a seat at his desk. After slight hesitation, he slid his bottom desk drawer open.

Letting out a large sigh, he began fishing through the drawer. As he began lifting a dime-size bag of marijuana out of the drawer, he caught a glimpse of a book beneath it. The words from his latest letter began ringing through his head: *"Maybe redemption has stories to tell. Maybe forgiveness is right where you fell. Where can you run to escape from yourself? Where you gonna go? Where you gonna go? Salvation is here."* Jason dropped the bag back into his drawer and took ahold of the book. He darted his blue eyes across the cover and ran his fingertips over its embossed letters. Then he wept.

Pastor Mark was reading at home in his office when he got the call. It was half past six on Tuesday evening, and the Robins had just finished dinner. It was not so much the words that Chris spoke as it was the urgency in his tone that made Pastor Mark's heart skip a beat. After hanging up the phone, he put down his book and rushed into the foyer.

"Helen, I have to go back to church," he called loudly to his wife in the nearby kitchen.

"Is something wrong?" Mrs. Robins asked, rushing into the foyer.

Pastor Mark swallowed deeply. "No, hunny. Don't worry. I'll be back in a little while," he replied and kissed his wife on the cheek before rushing out the front door.

Chris walked down the long hallway to Jason's bedroom, scared of what to expect. When Jason had called at five-thirty, Chris had just arrived home from football practice. Chris had never heard Jason speak so frantically. At first, he thought Jason might have been intoxicated. However, when Jason began reading Switchfoot lyrics, Chris realized that he was not high or drunk; he was sobbing.

Chris had seen Jason cry a few times; however, even at Andy's prayer service, Jason had not sobbed that uncontrollably. In fact, Chris had never heard Jason sound so distraught. Jason kept repeating the word "redemption" in a hysterical manner during their conversation. After twenty minutes of being unable to decipher what the issue was, Chris told Jason that he would come over.

Chris's mother had been putting dinner on the table when he got off the phone. She agreed to take him to the Davids' after they ate. Although it had only been forty-five minutes since Chris had hung up with Jason, it felt to Chris like it had been hours. He had called Pastor Mark on the drive to Jason's, and then begged his mother for a ride to the church. Chris tapped on Jason's door, hoping that he would not have to keep his mother waiting long. She had remained downstairs in the foyer, talking to Mrs. Davids.

"It's me, dude. Open up," Chris called and jiggled the locked doorknob.

Within three seconds, Jason flung his door open. Chris took one look at Jason and knew everything had finally come to a head. Jason had been bottling up his emotions about Cathy, Jessie, Andy, drugs, and God for the last three weeks. Jason had been doing an amazing job at handling everything, but God had prepared Chris for this very moment. Over the last three days, Chris's daily devotional readings had been about deliverance, salvation, and redemption. God had planned it perfectly that way. Stuff like that had begun happening quite often to Chris, which made him realize that there was no such thing as coincidence.

"Look at these!" Jason cried, thrusting three sheets of notebook paper at Chris.

Chris raised his eyebrows and took the papers from Jason. He began skimming one of the sheets. "These are lyrics to Switchfoot songs," he said as he flipped from one sheet to the next. "Did Chantal give you these? It looks like her handwriting."

Jason's eyes grew wide, and he grabbed the sheets back from Chris. "Welcome to the fallout! Welcome to resistance. The tension is here, the tension is here, *between who you are and who you could be,* between how it is and how it should be. I dare you to move," he read off as he took a seat on his bed. "I haven't told anyone about what I'm going through! How did she know? If these notes are from Chantal, how did she know how I was feeling? She couldn't have."

Chris pulled Jason's chair out from his desk and took a seat. "You're right," he said. "She can't know."

"Is this true?" Jason asked, picking a maroon leather book off of his bed and throwing it at Chris.

"The Bible?" Chris asked, shocked that Jason had one in his bedroom.

"Yeah, what it says about becoming a new creation and old things passing away," Jason stated, still looking and sounding distraught.

"That's what happened to me," Chris replied. "You've read some of the Bible?" he asked in bewilderment.

Jason nodded. "If it's true, then how did God write it?" Jason asked.

"All sixty-six books in the Bible were inspired by God. Whether they were written by prophets of the Old Testament—people who directly heard from God—or by disciples of Jesus Christ, all that is written is from God," Chris said, hoping that Jason would take him seriously. "There is a lot of historical evidence that backs up what is written, and there are no contradictions among the books."

"So, when you say people heard from God, what do you mean?" Jason asked.

"It says right in here that Christ's sheep know His voice," Chris stated and turned to the Gospel of John.

"Yeah, I read that," Jason said and took the Bible out of Chris's hand. "I came home after Andy's prayer service, and I read the Gospel of John. During the whole drive home from the service, I thought about the light that I saw shinning from Jessie and the difference I saw in you. Then I started thinking about the darkness that surrounded Cathy and me. It was like, all of a sudden, I could see things more clearly—things that I had never seen before. I couldn't understand it, but I couldn't deny the light. So, I came home and dug out this Bible. I turned to the Gospel of John rather than Matthew, Mark, or Luke because I had already heard enough from Pastor Mark that day, and I wasn't feeling my brothers' names. I almost died when I read the first five lines of John 1. It spoke of everything that I had just realized in the car," he said and handed Chris the book.

"In the beginning was the Word and the Word was with God, and the Word was God. He was in the beginning with God. All things were made through Him and without Him nothing was made

135

that was made. In Him was life, and the life was the light of men. And the light shines in the darkness, and the darkness did not comprehend it," Chris read, trying to process that he was actually reading from the *Bible* in Jason's bedroom.

"I felt like it couldn't have been a coincidence," Jason said. "Out of all the books in the Bible, I had turned to John. I looked after at the other Gospel's, and none of them start out like that. It was almost as if God was confirming my thoughts to me. Is that one way God speaks to people?"

Chris stared at Jason in disbelief. "Yeah, God speaks to us through his Word," he said once he found his voice. "You can read something in here twenty-five times, and it can speak to you in a different way each time."

"I believe you," Jason admitted. "You once said that you got strength from God to give up drugs. Pastor Mark told me the same thing. How did you guys get that much strength? I'm trying, but I'm slipping."

Chris bit his bottom lip in thought. "You know what, Jay?" he said after a moment. "I'm going to let Pastor Mark tell you."

Chapter 31

On Jason and Chris's drive to the church, Chris's cell phone began ringing. "Chris, I have to tell you something!" Chantal's voice rang through the phone as soon as Chris answered it. "Jason's been on my heart so heavily lately that I've been in constant prayer for him. I really think our prayers Friday night helped because he's been acting differently ever since. Jon told me that Jason said he's seeing things from a different perspective and has no idea why. I think God is working, Chris! I really think He is!"

"I think so, too," Chris replied, trying not to laugh.

"You're probably going to think this is weird, but I'm going to tell you anyway," Chantal continued. "I was listening to Switchfoot the other night, and I had the sudden desire to leave the lyrics in Jason's locker. I've been doing it all week. I started with the first song on the CD, and then moved to the second. Today, I felt such an urgency that during computer class I looked up the lyrics to *Dare You to Move* and left them in his locker. He was in class with me when I wrote them down, and I felt like such a psycho! I mean, I don't even know him that well! I don't even know what's going on with him and Cathy or him and Jessie. I know there must be a reason for it if I had the desire to do that. Do you think he knows who Switchfoot is?"

Chris began laughing and glanced over at Jason.

"You think I'm crazy, don't you?" Chantal asked.

"No, I don't think you're crazy, and I doubt he knows who Switchfoot is," Chris replied after a moment.

Jason turned and looked at Chris with protruding eyes.

"Actually, he showed me the notes, and I thought they were from you," Chris continued. "I'm on my way to see Pastor Mark right now. Can I call you later?"

"Did you tell him that you thought they were from me?" Chantal asked, sounding nervous.

"Yeah, but don't worry about it. It's a good thing," Chris replied. "I'll explain later."

"Ah! OK, bye," Chantal sang.

"OK, there's more confirmation for you," Chris said to Jason as he put his phone in his pocket. "You know how I said God speaks to people?"

"Yeah, through the Bible," Jason replied, staring at Chris curiously. "Was that Chantal?"

"Yeah," Chris said. "God also speaks to people through the Holy Spirit."

"The Holy Spirit is the Helper, right?" Jason asked. "He was given to the disciples so they could remember the teachings of Jesus. I remember reading that."

Chris was impressed by Jason's memory, forgetting for a moment that Jason was an absolute genius. "Yeah, exactly," Chris replied. "When someone is baptized with the Holy Spirit, or born again, they receive that same Helper. When I became a Christian in September, I asked the Holy Spirit into my heart. It is through the Holy Spirit that God ministers to me, convicts me, and directs me."

"I always prayed, 'in the name of the Father, of the Son, and of the Holy Spirit,' but I never really thought about why," Jason admitted. "I don't know why I didn't look into it."

"Probably because you were just taught it as a tradition," Chris said.

"Probably," Jason said and glanced out the window.

"So, Chantal was directed by the Holy Spirit—who puts desires in the hearts of Christ's followers—to write those lyrics out for you," Chris explained. "She had no idea what you were going through, but that didn't matter; she was obedient to God, and look how you were affected."

Jason turned to Chris and stared at him blankly. "Unbelievable," he said and let out a loud sigh.

Pastor Mark sat in the church office, in deep prayer. God had been laying Chris and Jason heavily on his heart since the day of Andy's prayer service. He had praised God daily for the fruit that he saw coming from Chris's new relationship with Christ. He also praised God for the trials in his own life that had enabled him to minister to Chris. Chris was "on fire for the Lord," having the deep hunger for God that all Christians should desire. Pastor Mark finished praying and opened the journal that was on his desk. He began to write down his thoughts about Chris and Jason:

Humility is a biblical virtue, something America's modern culture has tainted. To the world, pride is the virtue and humility is the weakness. In God's eyes, pride is a sin, something that eventually leads to self-destruction and death. Pride was the sin that fueled Satan's rebellion, leading to his fall from heaven. With modern day society teaching the need for high self-esteem, it was rare for a non-Christian teenager to possess humility.

Humility is Chris's strong point, something that sets him apart from the others. His realization that he is nothing without God and can do nothing without God makes him available to be used by God. Chris is a fantastic example of God's grace, healing, mercy, and love.

Jason, on the other hand, grieves my heart. He is an exceptionally bright teenager who has been handed all that the world has to offer on a silver platter. I realized after my first conversation with Jason that he is dissatisfied with the world. Jason's desire to escape from reality by way of drug-induced pleasure is prevalent among people who do not know God.

People are always setting their sights on more money, a bigger house, a better job, a certain person, or a nicer car in hopes of becoming fulfilled. The truth is that human beings were created with a void inside of them, a place designed only for God. No material item or other person can fill the abyss. So many people waste years of their lives searching for fulfillment, while Christ is ever-present saying, "If anyone thirsts, let him come to Me and drink."

People make the fatal mistake of being too busy worshipping the things of the world to listen to the Word of God. That is why so many of the celebrities, who seem to have it all, find themselves checking in and out of rehab. When people conquer the world and realize they still have emptiness inside of them, they become discouraged. In actuality, they have three choices: one, to live the rest of their life empty and depressed; two, to turn to drugs in hope of temporary fulfillment; or three, to ask the Lord to fill the void inside of them with His Holy Spirit.

"And I will pray the Father, and He will give you another Helper, that He may abide with you forever—the Spirit of truth, whom the world cannot receive, because it neither sees Him nor knows Him; but you know Him, for he dwells within you and will be in you," God's Word promises. "The Spirit also helps in our weaknesses. For we do not know what we should pray for as we ought, but the Spirit himself makes intercession for us with groanings that cannot be uttered."

It is evident to me that God has a strong calling on Jason's life. Satan has a strong grip on Jason, keeping him in bondage to drugs and a slave to sin. I have been praying for God to lift Satan's veil from Jason's eyes, so Jason can see things for what they truly are.

After realizing that God laid Jason on my daughter's heart, I knew that God was doing a great work. Although Chris has not mentioned Jason to me during our weekly appointments, I was not surprised by Chris's sudden phone call. There is clearly a fierce spiritual battle being fought over Jason's soul.

Someone once told me beauty, humor, intelligence, and special talents could easily become curses instead of blessings. People tend to gather around the funny person of the crowd, because everyone enjoys a good laugh. That is no secret. The same goes with beauty. Beautiful people get a lot of attention because the human eye is naturally drawn to beauty. People with exceptional intelligence or an area of talent also draw attention to themselves through success. Satan knows that the people who get the most attention are going to have a following. That is how the blessings can become curses. Satan often goes full force after the beautiful, talented, funny, and highly intelligent ones, seeking them out for his kingdom. They would be powerful resources for him. They could keep many in his grip. Satan also knows that if these people were a part of God's kingdom, they would bring powerful opposition to his own kingdom. They could lead many of their followers to the Lord.

Jason, having scored near perfect on the state's standardized testing, is clearly brilliant. On top of that blessing, he

140

is well known for his humor, charisma, and flawless beauty. Someone as gifted as Jason is the type of person Satan sought after. Tempting Jason into drugs at such a young age has been a great ploy of his. Drugs are one of Satan's mighty weapons. Addiction and pleasure keep the captives in bondage. A captive held that tightly in bondage could only be delivered to freedom by the power of God in Christ Jesus.

Chapter 32

Jason and Chris met Pastor Mark inside the church's entrance hall. Jason had not even attempted to wipe his tear-streaked face. The tears he had shed were cried to God, something he felt no need to disguise.

"Let's go into my office," Pastor Mark said and gestured for the boys to follow after him.

Jason glanced at his surroundings, recalling how packed the church had been during Andy's prayer service. He remembered the light that had shone from Jessie and the supernatural warmth he had felt inside the sanctuary. That long day, four Saturdays ago, had ended up being more significant than Jason ever anticipated.

"Take a seat," Pastor Mark said as they entered his office.

When Jason sat down, his eyes locked on a picture of Jessie on Pastor Mark's desk. He smiled as he gazed at the picture. He still could not believe that she had eaten lunch with him. His preconceived notion of Christians had been wrong. Pastor Mark, Chris, Chantal, and Jessie had all given him more than just the time of day.

As Pastor Mark glanced over at Jason, Jason realized that he was still staring at Jessie's picture. Jason felt his face flush as he turned his attention to Pastor Mark.

"Do you know my daughter?" Pastor Mark asked, glancing from Jason to Jessie's picture.

"Yes, sir," Jason replied and nodded slightly. "We had the opportunity to eat lunch together today."

Pastor Mark's eyes grew wide. "She's a great kid, but you don't have to call me 'sir,'" he smiled.

"Oh, sorry," Jason said, unaware that he had done so.

"So, what's been going on Jay?" Pastor Mark asked, leaning back comfortably in his chair.

Jason let out a deep breath and glanced at Chris. Chris was eyeing him with the same curious look Pastor Mark was wearing. Jason leaned back slightly in his chair and crossed his arms. He let out another heavy sigh and then began explaining. "I went home after Andy's prayer service and read the Gospel of John. I feel like I got a lot out of it, stuff that applied to my life. What I read made sense to me, and it got me thinking. I like reading things that make me examine myself. So, I decided that I needed to make some lifestyle changes. At first, it was more like I knew I had to, but I didn't really want to. It was really hard, but I distanced myself from my girlfriend and tried to stay away from drugs. That lasted for a few days, but I got sucked right back in. It has been an ongoing battle since.

"A little over a week ago, I told Cathy that we needed to take a long break. She completely freaked out, but I stuck to my words. She was pulling me away from everything that I needed to straighten out my life. Since then, the ugliness of her character has been revealed to me. Actually, a lot of things have been becoming clear to me. I don't know if I walked around in a complete daze before, or what, but I had a really warped perception of my life. Granted, I haven't gotten high in nine days, so that could account for some of the added clarity, but I don't think that's it.

"Something's been going on with me, like with my attitude and desires. Suddenly, things that seemed appealing to me before just don't, and things that had never interested me before do. Like, good things—stuff like volunteering and being nice to people I don't even know. It's awesome, and I've finally realized what a jerk I've been for, well, basically my entire life. What's weird is that I never saw that before. Cathy always seemed sweet to me; I never thought I was mean to anyone; I didn't know people thought I was heartless; and I certainly never thought myself worthy of your daughter's attention.

"So, yeah, a lot's been going on with me. It just seems like the harder I try to stay away from drugs the more they pop up around me. Like this morning, my brother offered me a fake ID, a pass out of school for the day, a rave ticket, and a bottle full of ecstasy. Is that normal? Do fifteen-year-olds normally get offered that at seven in the morning? Not the last time I asked around.

"Then one of my friends—no one you know—asked me if I wanted to trip during class. I don't think the kid's ever tripped before in his life. I didn't even know how to respond to his offer. Drugs just

143

seem to be coming at me from all angles. Honestly, it's torture. I used to think I was a strong person, but now, I know I'm weak.

"When I got home, I wanted to curl into a ball and die. I felt so burnt out. A voice in my head kept saying, 'your entire school thinks you're a heartless, drug addict, cheater of a boyfriend. You should just slip back into the daze you'd been in for the past two years. None of that ever bothered you when you were high all the time.' It was awful. I was so close to packing a bowl that I actually had a dime bag in my hand. Then, I caught a glimpse of the Bible I keep in my drawer, and I dropped the bag. Something came over me, something I really can't explain, but I just knew at that moment, I was nothing without God. I was a weak, heartless, mean, twisted, empty, broken, confused, powerless teenager." *Holy crap. Did I really just admit all of that to Jessie's dad?* Jason felt somewhat panic stricken.

"Jay, I didn't really know what you were going through," Chris spoke up as he glanced from Pastor Mark to Jason, "but God laid you heavily on my heart. You probably had no idea, but when you were at Samson's on Friday night, me, Jon, Tal, Marielle, and Alyssa were praying for you."

"Huh?" Jason asked and glanced at Chris strangely.

"Tal, Jon, and I have been praying that God will remove Satan's veil from your eyes so you can see clearly," Chris continued. "We've been praying for God to soften your heart and reveal the truth to you. I'm somewhat amazed right now, because I underestimated the power of prayer."

"You said that your desires began to change?" Pastor Mark asked.

"Yeah, like recently," Jason replied. "Like, two days ago."

"What did you do over the weekend?" Pastor Mark questioned him. "If you don't mind me asking."

Uh oh, Jason thought. *Well, bye-bye, Jessie. Having lunch with you once was nice.* "Oh, I was sick most of the weekend because of Friday night," Jason began and rolled his eyes. "I went to Chris's game, decided that it was a good idea to drink a pint of vodka, and then ended up getting in a fight. Actually, I'm glad I got

144

in that fight because those kids should not have been harassing Jessie and Sarah."

"Wait, what?" Pastor Mark interrupted him. "My Jessie? What happened?"

"Oh, she didn't tell you?" Jason asked.

Pastor Mark shook his head.

"I was in line for pizza with my friend, and a few sophomores started hitting on Jessie and Sarah. The girls kept telling them to go away. One of the kids put his arm around Jessie and said something kind of perverted. It completely turned my stomach, and, the next thing I knew, I had the kid on the ground. Of course, his friends jumped in. Then my brother had to break it up. Those kids won't be bothering Jessie anymore. I can promise you that," Jason explained.

"I had no idea that Jessie was a concern of yours," Pastor Mark said and raised his eyebrows.

Once again, Jason felt his face flush. "Well, I respect her," he said after a moment and made direct eye contact with Pastor Mark.

"Uh-huh, well, we can talk about that later," Pastor Mark said and smiled slightly. "Finish telling me about your weekend."

"OK," Jason said, relieved that he no longer had to talk about Jessie. "So, after the game, my brother took me to a party. I was so stupid, but I felt like I had to live up to both of my older brothers. Now, Matt hates drugs, but he can handle his liquor. Luke is kind of the opposite; he rarely ever drinks, but he likes club drugs. So, after I drank a pint of vodka, I convinced Luke to give me Vicodin. Then Matt, who didn't know I took the painkillers or drank the vodka, decided to teach me how to play a drinking game. I ended up drinking eleven beers before I passed out in my own vomit. I'm so sorry you just had to hear that."

"So, not the best night of your life," Pastor Mark summed up.

"I got *real* sick," Jason emphasized. "Then Matt found out about the painkillers, and he laid into me. He got me thinking about why I even bother with drugs and how destructive they are. He sort of steered me onto the right path with the idea of giving back to life

145

instead of always trying to get stuff from it. It made a lot of sense to me, and I decided I wanted to look into volunteering somewhere. The next day I mentioned it to Chris, and I'm not going to lie, he seemed really startled."

"I had no idea what was going on with you," Chris stated, wide-eyed. "You just seemed all over the place."

"I'm sure I did," Jason said. "After I talked to you that night, I read more of the Bible. I decided to read in Matthew, because Matt's talk helped me so much. I read the part that said, 'Come to Me all you who labor and are heavy laden, and I will give you rest. Take My yoke upon you and learn from Me, for My yoke is easy and My burden is light.' I memorized that because it meant something to me.

"Before I fell asleep that night, I prayed. I apologized for being such a bad person and for all of the sin that had been dominating my life. I told God that I didn't want to live that way anymore and that I was going to try my hardest to straighten out. I asked Him for help. I apologized for what happened to Andy, and I asked for forgiveness. I also asked for guidance. Then, I thanked God for being so forgiving and for sending Jesus to die in my place. Then, I fell asleep," Jason explained. "I meant what I said."

"I think that explains why your desires started to change," Chris said and looked at Pastor Mark.

"Jason, do you believe that God sent His only Son, Jesus Christ, to die for your sins?" Pastor Mark asked.

"Yeah," Jason said flatly. "After reading the Gospel and seeing what has been going on in my life lately, how could I not? When I prayed, I told God I believed that."

Pastor Mark smiled. "So, when you said that you realized you were nothing without God, what did you mean?" he asked.

Jason bit his bottom lip. "I guess what I meant was that I needed the strength Chris told me about. He said that he got his strength from having a relationship with Christ. When he told me that, I thought he was crazy. I figured he was just being humble and didn't want praise for overcoming his problems. It wasn't until I tried to go straightedge that I realized how hard it was. I'm not trying to put Chris down, but he used to be even weaker to temptation than me. Plus, he was worse into drugs than me. So, I realized there had to be some truth behind what Chris claimed. That was why I read some more of the Bible. Like I said, I know that I am nothing without God. I want Him to make use of me. I've done nothing but destruct myself. I might be knowledgeable, but I'm pretty stupid."

Pastor Mark smiled widely. "The reason why your desires and perspective have begun to change is because you accepted Christ as your Savior. Whether you realized it or not, you became a Christian. The Holy Spirit has begun working inside you, opening your eyes to see things you've never seen before, putting desires in your heart, and taking desires out. See, a lot of people mistakenly think they have to clean up their act before coming to God. What they don't realize is that God does the cleaning. He asks everyone to come to Him as they are."

Jason sat in silence, trying to process Pastor Mark's words.

"Wow," Chris said and let out a heavy sigh.

"So, this is what you were trying to explain to me?" Jason asked a moment later, turning toward Chris. "I thought it was so weird, what was happening inside of me, but now I know exactly what you meant when we were talking on Courtney's balcony before Andy's service. I'm sorry, guy. I thought you were out of your mind back then."

Chris laughed. "I know."

"So, this is real," Jason stated and leaned back in his seat. "Unbelievable."

"I'm going to read you something," Pastor Mark said and took hold of a nearby Bible. He began reading, "I thank my God upon every remembrance of you, always in every prayer of mine making request for you all with joy, for your fellowship in the gospel from the first day until now, being confident of this very thing, that He who has begun a good work in you will complete it until the day of Jesus Christ."

"I like that," Jason concluded.

"I think you will come to like this book very much," Pastor Mark said. "Now, do you have any more questions for me that don't concern my daughter, or should we begin that discussion?"

"Or could we not?" Jason asked.

"I think we can save that talk for another time," Pastor Mark said and laughed. "Why don't you call for your ride? I'm going to call home. I ran out of the house in such a hurry that I think I might have worried my wife."

"We really appreciate it, Pastor Mark," Chris said earnestly. "This meant a lot."

"Give God the glory. It's my pleasure," Pastor Mark replied, bringing his phone to his ear. "Hi, Jessie, is Mom there?" he asked after a moment. "That's OK, will you tell her that I'll be home soon? I love you, too, sweetheart. Bye."

"Are you going to tell her that I was here?" Jason asked.

"Anything said here is always confidential on my end," Pastor Mark replied. "I do have a strange feeling, however, that she'd be delighted to hear your story. Perhaps you'd like to tell her."

"I can't believe I'm a Christian," Jason said. He laughed and shook his head.

"Don't you get that song now?" Chris asked while texting his mom for a ride home. "The Todd Agnew one I downloaded on your computer?"

"*Grace Like Rain*?" Jason asked.

Chris nodded.

"Sounds like me," Jason said and pointed his thumbs at his chest. "Lost. Found. Blind. See. Got it."

Chapter 33

On Wednesday morning, Matt drove Jason and Ally to school. Luke apparently was too sick from the previous day's shenanigans to even consider getting out of bed. After yesterday's ride to school, Jason had a deepened appreciation for Matt.

"So, JD, how do you want me to deal with Lisa?" Ally asked as she turned to face Jason, who was sitting in the backseat of Matt's Lexus. "I pulled her onto varsity so I could have her drug tested, but now, I might actually need her for competition. Missy skipped yesterday with Luke and a few of our other friends. I'm sure you heard all about it. Anyway, the word got around, and my coach is irate. If Missy fails a drug test, I have to suspend her from the squad. She's obviously going to fail. We're going to need a flier to replace her. I don't have the time to train Lisa, kick her off the squad, and then train someone else. We put Lisa up in a few stunts yesterday; she has a great smile, a loud voice, and enough beauty to score us extra points. Say the word and I'll have her drug tested today. If she fails, like you say she will, her cheerleading career will be nipped in the bud. But in all honesty, we could benefit from having her on the squad."

Jason sighed and shook his head. "You know what, Ally? It was immature of me to want her kicked off the squad. I bet that Cathy filled Lisa's head with lies about me, and that Lisa was just trying to stick up for Cathy. They're best friends. I'd do the same thing for Chris. Just do whatever you have to do for your competition. Jessie doesn't even care about the rumors, and neither do I. Infuse Lisa with your morals if you can. She's a cool girl; she's just going through a hard time and acting kind of stupid."

Ally smiled at Jason. "You're so cute, JD. You're starting to remind me of Matt."

Jason raised his eyebrows and nodded. "Thanks," he said, savoring her words.

Chapter 34

As Chantal stepped out of her homeroom, she felt someone grab onto her arm. "Chantal!" Jason exclaimed loudly.

"Hey! You scared me," Chantal said as she allowed Jason to pull her aside.

"I don't want to make you late for class, but I have to tell you something," Jason stated. He had on the widest smile Chantal had ever seen him wear. She eyed him curiously, hoping that he was not on some sort of upper. "Thank you so much for leaving me those notes," he said. "You'll never know how much they impacted me."

Chantal let out a sigh of relief. He sounded sincere and perfectly sober. "So, you don't think I'm weird?" she asked and raised her eyebrows.

"No!" Jason assured her. "The last song you left me—the one that talks about the tension between who you are and who you could be—went through every emotion I was feeling. I know you have no idea what I'm talking about, or what I've been going through lately, but I want you to know that I appreciate everything. Actually, I think what you did was amazing. You know what? I think you're amazing, too."

Chantal laughed. "Well, OK. I can deal with that."

"I have to run to English, but I'll see you at lunch!" Jason called and then dashed off toward his classroom.

Chantal cocked her head to the side as she watched Jason disappear into his classroom. "That was weird," she mumbled. She shook her head in confusion and walked toward her own classroom.

"What's the matter?" Jon asked as Chantal entered her history class.

She took a seat behind Jon and placed her arms across her chest. "Jay just waited for me outside of homeroom and told me that I am amazing," she replied after a moment.

"Well, we know he didn't mistake you for Cathy," Jon remarked. "That's kind of weird though."

Chantal nodded. "He seemed really happy. He was like 'Leslie' happy. Do you know what I mean?"

"What's going on, guys?" Chris asked as he took a seat beside Chantal.

"Chantal and I think Jason took some nitrous hits after homeroom," Jon joked.

Chris smiled. "Well, that makes sense," he said flatly.

"It made no sense," Chantal assured him and shook her head.

Chris leaned in toward Chantal and Jon. "Our prayers have been answered," he whispered.

"What?!" Chantal exclaimed loudly. She shook her head in confusion and brought her hand to her jaw. "Was he with you when I called?"

Chris nodded.

"You've got to be kidding me," Chantal said in disbelief. "Jason went to see Pastor Mark?"

"Yeah, my mom was driving us there when you called," Chris replied. "Wait until Jason tells you what has been going on. I'm one-hundred percent guilty of underestimating the power of prayer. I'm sure he'll tell you the story at lunch. You're going to die when you see how much those lyrics coincided with everything."

"What lyrics?" Jon asked.

"I left some Switchfoot lyrics anonymously in Jason's locker," Chantal said, feeling her cheeks grow flush. "I felt like a creeper."

"Wait, so does this mean Jay's going to start coming to church?" Jon questioned Chris.

Chris shrugged. "I hope so."

"Andy's going to wake up soon," Chantal concluded. "I've known all along that God was doing something huge amongst our friends. Jason became a Christian? Now that's a *miracle*."

Jon and Chris nodded. They smiled back at Chantal. She found comfort in the hope she saw shining in their eyes.

"Can't you see the good that has come from Andy's accident?" Chantal asked. "Jay and Chris mended their friendship, Jon, you and I talked out our issues, Alyssa and I became friends again, you went back to church, Alyssa and Marielle started going to church, Chris and Jay got to know Pastor Mark, Jay somehow met Jessie, you and Alyssa became friends again, and Jay stopped doing

151

drugs and broke up with Cathy. Can't you see what's been happening? I bet there's so much we can't even comprehend," she rattled off in amazement.

"That's some good stuff," Jon agreed.

"I think you're right," Chris said. "I think Andy's going to wake up real soon."

Chapter 35

Jason darted his eyes around the cafeteria, looking for Jessie. He wanted to invite her to sit with him and his friends. He wanted her to hear the story that he was going to tell. Jessie had been the "thing" he had spoken of to Chris—the thing that caught his attention a few weeks back. She had inspired him, but he knew it went deeper than that. He had been drawn to her since Andy's prayer service in a completely non-physical way.

Jason felt someone tap on his shoulder. He turned around to see Jessie, smiling brightly at him. Jason smiled back at her, finding the innocent glow of her face beautiful. "Would you like to eat lunch with us today?" Jason asked and nodded toward his table.

"Sure," Jessie said. "But I have a present to give you first."

"A present?" Jason questioned her and let out a surprised laugh.

Jessie nodded and smiled widely. She reached into her backpack and pulled out a small red package.

"Do I need to open it here, or can I open it at the table?" Jason asked as he took the present from her hands.

"Whatever works," Jessie said with a shrug.

"Let's go sit down," Jason proposed, taking Jessie by the arm and leading her toward his table.

"Hi, Jessie!" Chantal greeted her warmly, as she and Jason sat down.

"Hi, Chantal. Hi, everybody," Jessie said quietly.

"Ooh, what do you have there, Jay?" Marielle asked as she leaned across the table to glance at his present.

"Jessie got me a present," Jason said and raised his eyebrows up and down.

"Aww, that's so nice!" Marielle cried.

"Can I open it?" Jason asked quietly and turned toward Jessie.

"Well, yeah," Jessie giggled.

Jason tore off the crimson wrapping paper and tossed it to the side. He glanced down at the present and raised his eyebrows.

He widened his eyes as soon as he realized what he was holding. "You've got to be kidding me!" he exclaimed. He laughed as he flipped over the CD to read its song list. "You got me a Switchfoot CD?"

"No way!" Chantal cried and widened her bright green eyes.

"This is the one!" Jason exclaimed in disbelief. "*Dare You to Move* is number five."

"That's crazy," Chantal said and shook her head.

"I don't get what's going on, guys," Jessie spoke up. She darted her blue eyes from Jason to Chantal.

"You didn't even know about the notes, huh?" Jason asked and glanced at Jessie.

"What are you talking about?" Jessie questioned him as she lowered her eyebrows.

"Dude, she couldn't have. We didn't even tell Pastor Mark about those last night," Chris stated.

"You saw my dad last night?" Jessie asked.

"When did you buy this?" Jason inquired of her.

"I bought it on Sunday. Actually, I bumped into Chris when I was buying it," Jessie replied.

"Oh yeah," Chris chuckled.

Jason glanced from Jessie to Chris and dropped his jaw. "Does stuff like this always happen to Christians?" he asked.

"Christians?" Jessie asked and glanced strangely at Jason.

Jason smiled.

"God works all things together for good to those who love Him," Chris stated and winked at Chantal.

Chapter 36

Wednesday night, Chantal walked into church with her parents and Stephanie. As Stephanie ran off toward her AWANA classroom and her parents began conversing with the usher, Chantal made a beeline for the sanctuary. Making her way to the left side of the room, she spied out Chris, Jon, and Jason sitting together near the altar. She hustled toward them and sat down beside Jon.

"So, Jay, are you excited to hear Jessie sing?" Chantal teased him as she reached across Jon and tapped Jason on the arm.

"Oh, like you're not," Jason replied with a short laugh.

"Any news on Andy?" Chris asked with a look of genuine concern in his baby-blue eyes.

"I just talked to his mom on the way here. She said nothing's changed for the better or worse," Chantal replied and put her head down. "I'm going to visit him tomorrow with Lisa."

"I was thinking about going to see him tomorrow, too," Jon said and placed his hand upon Chantal's shoulder.

"Thanks," Chantal said, trying to muster up a small smile. "I know he's going to pull through. I can feel it in my heart," she said and put her hand over her heart. She felt the sting of tears in her eyes.

"Come here," Jon sang compassionately and pulled her toward him.

Chantal rested her head on Jon's shoulder and began to sob.

"Do you want to pray?" Chris asked.

Chantal looked up at him and nodded slightly.

Chantal, Jon, and Jason bowed their heads as Chris began praying quietly. "Dear Lord, I lift Chantal up to You, and I ask You to please calm her spirit," he said. "She has been such an inspiration to so many of us and such an example of faith. Please fill her with Your peace that surpasses all understanding and continue to give her the faith to trust in You. Thank You so much for working in our hearts. It is a miracle that I am even sitting here tonight. Thank You for hearing our prayers and drawing Jason to You. You are awesome.

155

"Lord, I lift Andy up to You, and I ask that You place Your healing hand upon him. You are the great, all-knowing, all-mighty physician. If it is Your will, I pray that Andy wakes up from a coma soon without any complications. Please preserve the mental and physical abilities You have blessed him with. I thank You so much for Your Word that promises You work all things together for good to those who love You and are called according to Your purpose. I thank You and praise You for all the good that has come from this situation. I pray these things in Jesus' name, Amen."

Chantal lifted her head off of Jon's shoulder and glanced at Chris. "That was beautiful. Thank you," she said as she felt a tear drip off of her nose. "I just miss him."

"Just think about how surprised he's going to be when he wakes up," Jason said with a smirk as he patted Chantal's leg. "I bet he'll think he's still dreaming when he sees me in church."

Chantal smiled and rolled her eyes. "He's in for a few surprises," she agreed.

"Oh, Tal, I forgot!" Jason said, nearly jumping in his seat. "I have something for you," he added and handed her a card.

"What's this for?" Chantal questioned him as she wiped her face with the sleeve of her sweater.

"You'll see," Jason said.

Chantal took the blue envelope from Jason and began opening it. The worship team began gathering on stage, signaling that Bible study was about to begin. "I'll read this after," she whispered to Jason as the sanctuary lights began dimming.

The drummer, guitarist, bass player, and keyboardist began playing a few seconds before Jessie stepped up to the microphone. Chantal noticed Jason's eyes grow wide when Jessie began singing "All Who Are Thirsty" in her strong and steady voice.

Pastor Mark taught on Psalm 119:71-74. He spoke of God's sovereignty and how nothing happens to God's children that God has not allowed. Even Satan has to ask God's permission before he can do anything to a Christian. Pastor Mark pointed out that what Satan has meant for evil, God will work out for good. The hour-long message touched Chantal's heart and reminded her that God was involved in every detail of her life. By the end of the message, she was able to praise God for Andy's situation, accepting that it was part of God's perfect plan for Andy's life.

Chapter 37

It was a beautiful letdown when I crashed and burned
When I found myself alone unknown and hurt
It was a beautiful letdown the day I knew
That all the riches this world had to offer me would never do

In a world full of bitter pain and bitter doubts
I was trying so hard to fit, until I found out that
I don't belong here, I don't belong here
I will carry a cross and a song where I don't belong

It was a beautiful letdown when You found me here
Yeah, for once in a rare blue moon I see everything clear
I'll be a beautiful letdown that's what I'll forever be
And though it may cost my soul I'll sing for free
- Switchfoot

Chantal,
Thank you for your prayers and for being obedient to God. Thanks for caring about me, the lost black sheep walking around in darkness without a Shepherd. I'm sorry about Andy. I finally understand why God chose him, instead of me. You & Chris were right, God is in control & this is part of His plan. Thanks for pointing out the way God has been working in our lives & for being an example of His love. I suddenly have gained an eternal perspective, whereas before I couldn't see past myself. I guess I'm a Switchfoot fan now, too. Thanks for not following the crowd.
—Love, Jay

On Thursday afternoon, Lisa's brother drove Lisa, Chantal, Jon, and Leslie to visit Andy. When they arrived, Katherine and Bobby were sitting by Andy's bed. Bobby barely glanced up at them when they entered the room. Katherine was holding Bobby's hand and gazing at him sympathetically. Chantal could tell from Bobby's expression that he was losing hope.

God had given Chantal confirmation and encouragement that everything was going to turn out fine. How could she share that with Bobby? Seeing the pain in his eyes made her wish she could trade places with him to give him some of her faith. No one in the room besides Jon would have been open to hearing about God. Even though Leslie was Protestant, and Katherine and Bobby were Catholic, they never seemed to like it when Chantal mentioned Jesus.

Chantal knew Andy's friends thought she was weird. She realized that Andy's desire for popularity kept him from wholeheartedly walking with God. Andy often agreed with agnostic views just to blend in with the crowd. He was lukewarm, with one foot in and one foot out of the church. He had just enough of God to relate to Chantal and just enough of the world to appear impartial. Chantal knew Andy's position was a horrible place to be. What he had of the world made him not completely comfortable with God; what he had with God made him uncomfortable in the world. He was neither here nor there.

When Andy was away from his friends, he was a completely different person. He wanted to hear about what God was doing in Chantal's life. He wanted to pray with her. Sometimes, he would even email her scripture. As Chantal stared at Andy's blank face she thought, *who are you?* With her whole heart, she wanted to believe that the side of Andy she saw when they were alone was the real Andy. She wanted to believe that who he was around his friends was a just a front.

How could anyone be best friends with Lisa and in a relationship with Chantal? Would Satan and Jesus make a cozy household? No! Chantal knew that there was no in between. Anyone who wasn't *for* Jesus Christ was *for* Satan. Chantal knew that was a bold and true statement. She also knew one of Satan's tactics was to make people believe they could remain impartial and not face judgment. It was a great lie of his; it kept people from realizing that they were part of his kingdom. In truth, anyone who wasn't walking in the light was, in fact, walking in darkness. Chantal glanced around the room at Andy's friends, wondering if they would ever understand that.

After a moment, Chantal walked over to Andy's bed and affectionately touched his face. How had she allowed herself to fall in love with a stumbling block? Chantal wanted Andy to wake up as

159

much as anyone else did. She missed her boyfriend terribly, but their month apart had been a blessing for Chantal in many ways. She had realized how much Andy held her back from God. While Andy was in a coma, Chantal realized that he was not the spiritual leader she desired to have as a boyfriend.

Previously, she had thought dating a Christian was all that mattered. She had not realized two believers could be on completely different paths. Although Chantal had never seen two unequally yoked animals try to carry a heavy load, she could imagine the difficultly. Two animals tied together, running in opposite directions, were not going to get anywhere. She had feared for quite some time that God was trying to show her that she and Andy were those two animals. Ignoring that revelation had become a heavy burden on Chantal's heart.

Chantal had talked to Jon about her situation with Andy. She admitted that while most people were praying for Andy to wake up healthy, she had been praying for God to reveal to him the lukewarm temperature of his heart. It had been somewhat awkward for Chantal to confide in Jon about her relationship with Andy, but she knew Jon would give her Godly advice. Even though he had fallen off the straight and narrow path for a while, Jon was once again in the right place.

Jon's advice had been simple, but it was more valuable than a book's worth of worldly advice. "Chantal, maybe God has taken Andy away for a little while to ease the pain of a future breakup. You've already suffered through the separation anxiety, and you are used to him not being around. Just remember that you are married to Christ. You are His and His alone. If you feel like Andy is holding you back from furthering your walk with God, then you are unequally yoked. Jesus said, 'My burden is light.' If your relationship with Andy has become a heavy burden, then it is not of the Lord. When you are in His will there is fruit."

Jon's advice was valuable to Chantal; it confirmed what she already knew. She glanced down at Andy, praying for God to work a miracle in his heart. Chantal loved Andy, and she hated the idea of breaking up with him. She knelt down by Andy's side, took hold of his hand, and closed her eyes. Tears began streaming down her face as she prayed silently for their relationship.

"Chantal! Why can't I see you?" a faint voice called out, interrupting her prayer. Chantal shot her eyes open and planted them on Andy.

Leslie, Bobby, Katherine, Jon, and Lisa rushed to Andy's bedside.

"Did he just say something?" Katherine asked as she glanced from Andy to Chantal.

"He said he couldn't see me," Chantal replied, feeling her heart pound against her chest. "He said my name. Oh my gosh! He said my name! He remembered my name!"

"That's a really good sign," Leslie said.

"Should we go get the doctor?" Lisa asked.

"He must be dreaming about you," Bobby said.

Chantal smiled at Bobby, silently thanking God for Andy's sign of improvement. When she turned back to Andy, butterflies began fluttering around in her stomach.

Andy began creasing his eyelids open. Once his eyes were open, he locked them on Chantal. "Now I see you," he said quietly. Then he closed his eyes a second later and spread a peaceful smile across his lips.

Epilogue

Monday found me on my knees again, breathing you in
To blur the lines that mark where I begin, and where you end
No use in trying to pretend, come take me again
Cause rumor has it I'm not who I've been
Come define me
What can we do if the rumors are true?
I turn everything over I turn myself in
I turn everything over I turn myself in
There's nothing left of me to defend
I turn everything over I turn myself in
The evidence convicts the hollow man
After looking inside
To my dismay I find I'm just one of them
Cause I'm an already but not yet resurrected fallen man
Come break this limbo
And I know you know just who I've been
Come define me
What can we do if the rumors are true?
I turn everything over I turn myself in
- Switchfoot

"And a servant of the Lord must not quarrel but be gentle to all, able to teach, patient, in humility correcting those who are in opposition, if God will perhaps grant them repentance, so that they may know the truth, and that they may come to their senses and escape the snare of the devil, having been taken captive by him to do his will." – 2 Timothy 2:24-26

Jessie,

    I walked around dead for 15 years, in complete darkness. I had a veil over my eyes that made things appear bright and convinced me that I was alive. Then I saw you. I never realized that I was dead, until I saw the life and the light that shone from you. I knew that very moment that you had something I lacked. You had something I desperately needed. I had the world at my fingertips, but you had the truth. God reached me through you. Thank you for being the 2nd Timothy gentle, patient, and humble servant of the Lord. I was a captive, but God has set me free. I hope you remain in my life as the blessing you have already become in this short time. - Jason

"If anyone is in Christ, he is a new creation; old things have passed away; behold, all things have become new." – 2 Corinthians 5:17

Other Books by Stacy A. Padula

Gripped Part 1: The Truth We Never Told

In high school, Taylor Dunkin broke more records than any other athlete to step foot in Montgomery, Massachusetts. As a sophomore in college, he was ranked by ESPN as one of the NFL's top 100 prospects. However, his aspirations came to a jarring halt when a knee injury and two surgeries left him sidelined.

One year later, Taylor is a person of interest in a highly confidential investigation headed by the Boston Police Department. He has entangled himself in a crime ring notorious for pushing opiates, cocaine, and benzodiazepines on local college campuses. When Taylor's younger brother Marc discovers that Taylor is behind the copious drug supply circulating around Montgomery Lake High School, he sets off to not only reverse the damage Taylor has caused, but also save his lifelong role model from becoming a casualty of America's deadly opioid epidemic.

Gripped Part 2: Blindsided

Fourteen-year-old Chris Dunkin is known for being the life of the party and everyone's favorite friend. Despite his amicable nature, he carries around deep-seated pain from his childhood that he frequently numbs with alcohol and drugs.

After hosting a party, Chris awakes with a strange vibe running through his body and no recollection of the previous night. When he learns the horrifying truth of what his night entailed, the trajectory of his life is changed forever.

Montgomery Lake High #1: The Right Person

Growing up in the shadow of two NFL-destined cousins, Chris Dunkin has high hopes for his own future in football. However, a drug addiction threatens to destroy everything he has worked hard to attain. When Chris meets Courtney Angeletti—the mayor's straightedge Christian daughter—he believes she could be the source of inspiration he needs to overcome his destructive lifestyle. Courtney, however, has other ideas.

The desire to rebel has been tugging on Courtney's heartstrings for some time, and Chris's "bad-boy" reputation draws her to him like a moth to a flame. After all, he is a central part of the most popular clique in her high school. Will Chris pull Courtney away from her faith or will Courtney inspire him to overcome his rebellious lifestyle?

Montgomery Lake High #2: When Darkness Tries to Hide

Jason Davids has not slept in thirty-seven hours. He glances at his clock: 7:20 p.m.

You can do this, Jason, he says to himself. *Just get up and go. Go tell them the truth. Tell everyone at Alyssa's party that you found Andy's body. Tell them that he looked dead. Tell them about the horror in Chantal's eyes when she came rushing up the stairs. Make sure you tell them that it is all your fault.*

One day after a tornado strikes Montgomery, Massachusetts, Andy Rosetti is in a coma with life-threatening injuries. Jason Davids and Chris Dunkin devise a plan to help Andy and unite the students at Montgomery Lake High School. However, no one—not even Chris—knows Jason's secret about the day of the storm.

Montgomery Lake High #4: The Battle for Innocence

Jon Anderson and Chantal Kagelli are trying to live moral lives, but temptations are plaguing them in and out of school. Will they continue to be lights in their best friends' lives or will they get pulled into the darkness?

Montgomery Lake High #5: The Forces Within

After being trapped inside his own body, unable to communicate with anyone but his own thoughts, Andy Rosetti finally wakes up from the coma that controlled his life for one month. But upon awakening, Andy finds himself and his friends in an unfamiliar setting: a mansion riddled with secret passages and supernatural forces. As his friends fall prey to the entities surrounding them, Andy must figure out if the darkness lies within the mansion's walls or within the people surrounding him.

About the Author

Stacy A. Padula, a native of Pembroke, Massachusetts, has accrued years of experience working with adolescents. She has been a mentor, life coach, youth group leader, and private educational consultant with extensive experience in the fields of college counseling, tutoring, and standardized test preparation. She is the Founder and President of South Shore College Consulting & Tutoring based in Plymouth, Massachusetts.

Awards: Stacy was featured in Marquis Who's Who in America (2018) for excellence in literature and education, Marquis Who's Who in the World (2018 & 2019), and Cambridge Who's Who for Young Professionals (2009). In 2018, she was awarded the Albert Nelson Lifetime Achievement Award, and in 2019, the International Association of Top Professionals (IAOTP of New York, NY) chose Stacy as its "Top Educational Consultant of the Year." Each of her novels have risen to best seller status in a variety of categories on Amazon from 2010-2019. From February through March of 2019, "Gripped Part 1" was the #1 New Release on Amazon Kindle in its category. As a teenager, Stacy was a high honors student who graduated towards the top of her class at Silver Lake Regional High School. She was in National Honor Society and Who's Who Among American High School Students. She earned the Maxima Cum Laude/Silver Medal in the National Latin Exam, three Varsity letters, and the Louisa May Alcott Writing Award. Stacy was also a top-ten finalist in Miss Teen Southern New England and awarded the Academic Achievement Award for having the highest GPA out of all contestants.

Publications: Stacy's first novel, "The Right Person," was published in 2010. In 2011, "When Darkness Tries to Hide" was published, followed by "The Aftermath" (Padula's personal favorite) in 2013. In 2014, both "The Battle for Innocence" and "The Forces Within" were released, and in 2015, all five books hit the shelves of Barnes & Noble. For Stacy, it was a dream come true to see her books for sale in the popular, mainstream bookstore! In 2016, Barnes & Noble chose Stacy to be a featured author for its teen book festival. In 2019, she released a new book series called "Gripped," which chronicles how good kids become drug addicts. She is currently working on a screenplay adaptation of her novel "The Aftermath" and writing "Gripped Part 4."

Background: Stacy was a Presidential Scholar and on the Dean's List at Wentworth, where she studied Architecture and Interior Design. After graduation, she worked at an architecture firm in Boston for two years. Although she enjoyed her work, she felt something was missing—she wanted to spend more time helping people grow academically and spiritually. For close to a year, she split her time between tutoring, writing, and working at a design firm in Plymouth. When she fell in love with tutoring, she left the A&D industry completely and took a full-time position with an educational company. She attained tutoring certification in 2009 through The International Tutor Association. Her career took off, and within one year, she was promoted to Program Director. Stacy knew she had found her niche! During her eight years with that company, she received multiple promotions and held a variety of titles, including Manager of Curriculum & Instruction and Director of Operations. In 2016, Stacy founded South Shore College Consulting & Tutoring. Then in 2019, she founded Briley & Baxter Publications—a publishing company that uses part of its monthly proceeds to support animal rescues. Stacy is currently enrolled in the University of Pennsylvania Wharton School's online Entrepreneurship Specialization to pursue her passion for business. In her spare time, she enjoys skiing, attending Bruins games, reading about psychology, taking her dogs to the beach, and spending time with her family, husband Tim, and friends. Stacy writes young adult novels in the hopes of preparing teens to face the "war zone" that is high school—to help kids deal with the stress and peer pressure and to encourage them to "steer a straight path, pursue God, and not fall for the false promises of the world."

Connect with Us!

Stacy's Instagram @author_stacypadula
Stacy's Twitter @MLHBookSeries
Cathy's Instagram @ckagelli99
Chantal's Instagram @chantal_kagelli
Jason's Instagram @jds_on
Lisa's Instagram @lisa_ankerman99
Chris's Instagram @dunkin_85
Luke's Instagram @lukedavids97
Alyssa's Instagram @alyssa_kelly02
www.stacyapadula.com
www.brileybaxterbooks.com
www.highambition.org

Did You Enjoy MLH #3?

If you loved this book, would you leave a review on Amazon?

Lightning Source UK Ltd.
Milton Keynes UK
UKHW012337170620
365183UK00007B/230